O9-AIF-576

From: Nannie

Engaging
Father Christmas

Engaging Father Christmas

A NOVELLA

Robin Jones Gunn

NEW YORK BOSTON NASHVILLE

This book is a work of fiction. Names, characters, places, and incidents are the product of the author's imagination or are used fictitiously. Any resemblance to actual events, locales, or persons, living or dead, is coincidental.

Copyright © 2008 by Robin's Ink, LLC.
All rights reserved. Except as permitted under the U.S. Copyright Act of 1976, no part of this publication may be reproduced, distributed, or transmitted in any form or by any means, or stored in a database or retrieval system, without the prior written permission of the publisher.

Unless otherwise indicated, Scriptures are taken from the HOLY BIBLE: NEW INTERNATIONAL VERSION®. Copyright © 1973, 1978, 1984 by International Bible Society. Used by permission of Zondervan Publishing House. All rights reserved.

FaithWords
Hachette Book Group USA
237 Park Avenue
New York, NY 10017

Visit our Web site at www.faithwords.com.
FaithWords is a division of Hachette Book Group USA, Inc.
The FaithWords name and logo are trademarks of Hachette Book Group USA, Inc.

Book design by Fearn Cutler de Vicq

Printed in the United States of America

First Edition: October 2008
10 9 8 7 6 5 4 3 2 1

Library of Congress Cataloging-in-Publication Data
Gunn, Robin Jones
Engaging Father Christmas / Robin Jones Gunn. — 1st ed.
p. cm.
Summary: "Robin Jones Gunn charms readers with this poignant novella about a woman searching for love, and finding so much more in the arms of a certain Father Christmas this holiday season"—Provided by the publisher.
ISBN-13: 978-0-446-17946-1
ISBN-10: 0-446-17946-9
1. Christmas stories.   I. Title.
PS3557.U4866E64 2008
813'.54—dc22   2008022271

For Janet and Paula,
who gifted me with peace and grace throughout the journey.

Acknowledgments

A warm thank-you goes to those who make this adventure of storytelling a joy and a privilege: my agent, Janet Kobobel Grant, who always believes "everything will work out"; my patient and ever-encouraging husband, Ross; our equally supportive children, Ross and Rachel; my fabulous assistant, Rachel Zurakowski; my PPC writing pals, Jaynie and Meg; and my editor, Anne Horch, along with the entire team at FaithWords. Thanks for all the ways each of you makes me smile and nudges me forward as a writer and friend. I'm deeply grateful for you.

Engaging
Father Christmas

"For I know the plans I have for you," declares the LORD, "plans to prosper you and not to harm you, plans to give you hope and a future."

Jeremiah 29:11

Chapter One

*a*round me swarms of Londoners rushed by, intent on their destinations and sure of their plans. My destination was the small town of Carlton Heath, and my plans revolved around a certain Scotsman who was now officially late.

I tried to call Ian again. His voice mail picked up for the third time. "It's me again," I said to the phone. "I'm here at Paddington station and—"

Before I finished the message, my phone beeped, and the screen showed me it was Ian.

"Hi! I was just leaving you another message." I brushed back my shoulder-length brown hair and stood a little straighter, just as I would have if Ian were standing in front of me.

"You made it to the station, then?"

"Yes. Although I was about to put on a pair of red rain boots and a tag on my coat that read, 'Please look after this bear.' " I was pretty sure Ian would catch my reference to the original

Paddington Bear in the floppy hat since that was what he had given to my niece, Julia, for Christmas last year.

"Don't go hangin' any tags on your coat," Ian said with an unmistakable grin in his voice. "I'm nearly there. The shops were crammed this morning, and traffic is awful. I should have taken the tube, but I'm in a taxi now. I'll be there in fifteen minutes tops. Maybe less if I get out and run the last few blocks."

"Don't run. I'll wait. It's only been, what? Seven weeks and three days since we were last together? What's another fifteen minutes?"

"I'll tell you what another fifteen minutes is. It's just about the longest fifteen minutes of my life."

"Mine too." I felt my face warming.

"You're at track five, then, as we planned?"

"Yes. Track five."

"Good. No troubles coming in from the airport?"

"No. Everything went fine at Heathrow. The fog delayed my flight when we left San Francisco, but the pilot somehow managed to make up time in the air. We landed on schedule."

"Let's hope my cabbie can find the same tailwind your pilot did and deliver me to the station on schedule."

I looked up at the large electronic schedule board overhead, just to make sure my watch was in sync with local time. "We have about twenty minutes before the 1:37 train leaves for Carlton Heath. I think we can still make it."

"I have no doubt. Looks like we have a break in the traffic jam at the moment. Don't go anywhere, Miranda. I'll be there as soon as I can."

"I'll be here."

I closed my phone and smiled. Whenever Ian said my name, with a rolling of the r, he promptly melted my heart. Every single time. His native Scottish accent had become distilled during the past decade as a result of his two years of grad school in Canada and working in an architect office with coworkers from around the world. But Ian knew how to put on the "heather in the highlands" lilt whenever he wanted. And I loved it, just as I loved everything about this indomitable man.

I looked around the landing between the train tracks for an open seat on one of the benches. Since none were available, I moved closer to the nearest bench just in case someone decided to leave.

Balancing my large, wheeled suitcase against a pole so it wouldn't tip over, I carefully leaned my second bag next to the beast. This was my third trip to England since my visit last Christmas and the first time I had come with two suitcases. This time I needed an extra bag for all the gifts I had with me, wrapped and ready to go under the Christmas tree at the Whitcombe manor.

Last Christmas and for many Christmases before that, the only gift I bought and gave was the one expected for the exchange at the accounting office where I worked in downtown San Francisco. Up until last Christmas I had no family to speak of — no parents, no siblings, no roommate. I didn't even have a cat. My life had fallen into a steady, predictable rhythm of work and weekends alone, which is probably why I found the courage to make that first trip to Carlton Heath last December. In those brief, snow-kissed, extraordinary few days,

I was gifted with blood relatives, new friends, and sweetest of all, Ian.

Christmas shopping this year had been a new experience. While my coworkers complained about the crowds and hassle, I quietly reveled in the thought that I actually had someone — many someones — in my life to go gift hunting for.

I had a feeling some last-minute shopping was the reason Ian was late. He told me yesterday he had a final gift to pick up this morning on his way to the station. He hadn't explained what the gift was or whom it was for. His silence on the matter led me to wonder as I wandered along a familiar path in my imagination. That path led straight to my heart, and along that path I saw nothing but hope for our future together — hope and maybe a little something shiny that came in a small box and fit on a certain rather available finger on my left hand.

Before my mind could sufficiently detour to the happy land of "What's next?", I heard someone call my name. It was a familiar male voice, but not Ian's.

I looked into the passing stream of travelers, and there he stood, only a few feet away. Josh. The last person I ever expected to see again. Especially in England.

"Miranda, I thought that was you! Hey, how are you?" With a large travel bag strapped over his shoulder, Josh gave me an awkward, clunking and bumping sort of hug. His glasses smashed against the side of my head. He quickly introduced me as his "old girlfriend" to the three guys with him.

"What are you doing here?" He unstrapped the bag and dropped it at his feet.

One of the guys tagged his shoulder and said, "We'll be at the sandwich stand over there."

"Okay. I'll be there in a few minutes." Josh turned back to me. "You look great. What's been happening with you?"

"I'm good," I said. "What about you? What are you doing here?" I was still too flustered at the unexpected encounter to jump right into a catch-up sort of conversation after the almost three-year gap.

"Just returned from a ski trip to Austria with a group from work. Incredible trip. I'm in a counseling practice now. Child psychologist. I don't know if you knew that."

"No. That's great, Josh. I know that's what you wanted to do."

"Yes, it's going well so far." He seemed at ease. None of the stiltedness that had been there right after I broke up with him came across in his voice or demeanor.

"And what about you? What are you doing in England?"

Before I could put together an answer, Josh snapped his fingers. "Wait! Are you here because you're looking for your birth father?"

"You remembered." Once again he surprised me.

"Of course I remembered. You had that picture of some guy dressed as Father Christmas, and it had the name of the photography studio on the back. That was your only clue."

I nodded.

"So? What happened?"

"I followed the clue last Christmas, and it led me here, to my birth father, just like you thought it would."

"No way! Did it really?"

I nodded, knowing Josh would appreciate this next part of the story. "The man in the photo dressed like Father Christmas was my father. And the boy on his lap is my brother, or I guess I should say my half brother, Edward."

"Incredible," Josh said with a satisfied, Sherlock Holmes expression on his unshaven face. "What happened when you met him?"

I hesitated. Having not repeated this story to anyone since it all unfolded a year ago, I didn't realize how much the answer to Josh's question would catch in my spirit and feel sharply painful when it was spoken aloud.

"I didn't meet him. He passed away a few years ago."

"Oh." Josh's expression softened.

"You know, Josh, I always wanted to thank you for the way you urged me to follow that one small clue. I've wished more than once that I would have come to England when you first suggested it four years ago. He was still alive then. That's what I should have done."

"And I should have gone with you," he said in a low voice.

"Why do you say that?"

Josh's eyebrows furrowed, his counselor mode kicking in. "I felt you needed that piece in your life. By that I mean the paternal piece of your life puzzle. I didn't like you being so alone in the world. I wish you could have met him."

"I do, too, but I actually think things turned out better this way. It's less complicated that I didn't meet him while he was still alive."

"Why do you say that?" Josh asked.

I hesitated before giving Josh the next piece of information.

In an odd way, it felt as if he needed the final piece of the puzzle the same way I had.

"It's less complicated this way because my father was..." I lowered my voice and looked at him so he could read the truth in my clear blue eyes. "My father was Sir James Whitcombe."

Chapter Two

osh slowly leaned back, stunned. He raised an eyebrow and let out a low whistle. "I can see what you mean about its being complicated. No one will want to believe Sir James had a child outside of his reportedly idyllic marriage. Except the tabloids, of course. He was an incredible actor, you know."

"Yes, I know."

I realized we were in a noisy, crowded train terminal, but I still didn't want to take any chance of being overheard. Leaning closer and lowering my voice I said, "Only a few people know, so please don't say anything to anyone."

"I understand. Don't worry. Holding onto confidences is what I do for a living." Josh reached over and gave my shoulder a squeeze.

"I really mean it, Josh. If the truth got out, it would damage the lives of some people I really care about."

"I hear what you're saying. You can trust me, Miranda. I

think you know that. But in my experience as a counselor, I've found that truth has a way of rising to the surface. Sometimes you must wait for the truth to float to the top. Other times you must go to it, take it by the hand, and pull it up with all your might."

Josh's summary statement was typical of the way many of our conversations went when we were together. To me, he often sounded as if he had read one too many motivational books on inner healing.

An older gentleman who had been sitting on the bench behind me stepped around to the side and said, "Pardon me." He turned his cell phone away from his ear, and stepping closer he pointed at the open seat and said, "Were you waiting for a place to sit?"

"Yes. Thank you."

He tipped his cap and walked away.

"I'd better go." Josh glanced to where his friends had congregated, waiting for him. "Listen, here's my card. Call me if you want. Any time. I'd like to keep in touch."

"Thanks."

"Do you live here now?" Josh picked up his heavy bag and threw it over his shoulder. "In England, I mean."

"No. Not yet. I hope to move here when . . . well, soon."

"My e-mail is on the card too. Merry Christmas, and again, Miranda, I'm really glad you connected with your family. You needed that." He leaned over and gave me a kiss on the cheek.

I was watching Josh walk away when I heard another familiar male voice behind me. This voice was the one I heard in my dreams. All the good dreams that included a white wedding dress and a cottage in the glen.

My Scotsman had arrived.

"So, that's how it is, is it?" Ian MacGregor stood there with his fists on his hips. "I ask you to wait on me for a quarter of an hour, and you take to giving out kisses to the first man in a ski cap who comes your way. What was he peddling? Mistletoe, was it?"

I turned to Ian slowly, enjoying the chance to play along with his teasing. "Those are the chances you take when you leave a woman waiting, you know."

Ian's eyes lit up at the sight of me. His light brown hair looked windblown, and his handsome face had a ruddy glow. I tumbled into his arms and gave him the kiss I'd been saving for seven weeks and three days. Then he gave me the kiss he had been saving for seven weeks and three days. It was the best Christmas gift exchange ever.

I think we might have kept kissing, except our train had arrived and passengers were boarding. As we drew apart from our tight embrace, my watch caught on the strap of the messenger bag Ian used in lieu of a briefcase. I pulled it off his arm.

In the fumble to untangle ourselves, the bag tipped open, spilling his car keys, cell phone, and an old-fashioned, ivory jewelry box just large enough for a diamond ring.

Ian knelt down to gather up the items, and I knelt right along with him, trying to unclasp my wristwatch. Our faces were inches apart as he hurriedly tucked the jewelry box in his coat pocket and turned with a shy expression as if to see if I'd noticed.

Of course I'd noticed. What should I say?

Without hesitation, the truest impulse on my heart strode

right to the edge of my lips and did a lovely swan dive into the deep end as I said, "Yes?"

Ian gave me one of his fake growls. "I haven't asked you yet, woman."

"Asked me what?" I said, equal to his mock naiveté.

He kissed me soundly. "I believe you and I have a train to catch."

Chapter Three

 love the train ride to Carlton Heath. But I loved it more that afternoon because I was cozied up next to Ian, and both of us were smiling. I'm sure that to observers our grins were sophomoric and comical. I don't know about Ian, but I couldn't make my face behave seriously.

Neither of us spoke for the first little while as the train rolled out of the station. We sat close and settled in, remembering how it felt to have our arms linked and our fingers laced together. I leaned my head on Ian's broad shoulder and released a contented sigh. He kissed the top of my head.

His cell phone rang. He let it go unanswered.

"I'm ready to hear your confession," Ian mumbled in my ear.

"My confession?" I sat up and looked at him. "Do you mean you want to know who the mistletoe peddler was in the ski cap?"

"Yes. Go on."

"That was Josh. My old boyfriend. I've told you about him."

"And what was he doing at Paddington? He doesn't live here, does he?"

"No. He was on a ski trip to Austria."

"Is that it?"

"You mean is that all I have to say?"

"Yes. Is that it?"

"Yes. That's it, Ian. If you had arrived a few minutes earlier, I would have introduced you to each other."

"And if I had arrived a few minutes earlier, I would have —"

Before Ian could issue me a benediction of constant protection, his cell phone rang. Once again he ignored it. I had a feeling that was because his phone was in his coat pocket along with "the box." He seemed intent on ignoring the box for the moment.

"Actually, I do have one more thing to say about seeing Josh."

"So, there is more," Ian said.

"Not much more. What I wanted to add is that, even though it was strange seeing Josh after all these years, I'm glad I did. It always felt as if that relationship needed the final dots connected."

"And are they connected now?"

I smiled at him and nodded. "Yes."

His phone rang a third time. Ian gingerly pulled it from his coat pocket without also extracting "the box" and looked at the screen. "It's Katharine. I'll put her to rest and let her know we're on our way."

Katharine, the tall, gentle-spirited woman who married Ian's father, Andrew, two years ago, had been a kind friend to me on my first visit to Carlton Heath. She and Andrew ran a small place called the Tea Cosy. That's where I first entered the circle of friends I now called my own.

"Hello, Katharine. I'm with Miranda now, and we're on the train."

As he listened to her response, Ian pulled away from our relaxed position and sat up straight.

"Katharine, your voice cut out for a moment. Did you say heart attack?"

He listened carefully and checked his watch. "My car is at the station, so we'll go directly to hospital. Tell him we're on our way."

Ian closed his phone and turned to me with a stunned expression.

"Your dad?"

He nodded.

"What did Katharine say?"

"The doctor is referring to it as an 'episode.' They've run tests and are waiting for results."

Ian rose and said, "Wait here."

With determined strides he went to the automatic door that opened between the train cars and headed toward the front of the train. I knew that, if it were at all possible, he would convince the conductor to break a speed record in reaching Carlton Heath.

I felt my heart pounding as I checked my cell phone and saw that I had two missed calls from Katharine. My phone must have been temporarily out of range when she tried to reach us. She hadn't left a message, so I didn't have any further details. My first response was to try calling her back, but when I did, she didn't pick up.

I sat with my phone in my lap, blinking and trying to sort out the implications of this unwanted news. *Please don't take him, God. Not now. Not at Christmas. Not this Christmas. We need Andrew in this world.*

I fixed my numbed gaze on a box held protectively in the lap of a woman the next aisle over. The picture on the box was of a nativity scene. All the key players were present: Mary, Joseph, baby Jesus, three wise men, two shepherds, a lamb, and a donkey. The fully set stage reminded me of my mother, and instantly thoughts of her bombarded me.

My mother, who always referred to herself as "Eve Carson the Actress," was big on curtain calls. She loved it when all the key players were on stage together, ready for their accolades. Her curtain call on life came far too soon, and there definitely was no applause at her passing. I was her only daughter, and she was my gypsy mother.

I remember exactly where I was sitting the moment one of the stagehands in Salinas came to tell me of her fall at the dress rehearsal for *The Merchant of Venice.* I was eleven years old, and my favorite place to make myself invisible was backstage in the wardrobe room. I could always find a trunk to use as a couch and an unused coat to fold into a pillow. My companion in that private boudoir was always a book.

Sometimes I'd fall asleep there. Other times the seam-stress would slip me peppermints she had lifted from the supply set aside for the actors to help clear their throats before performances.

My mother knew where to find me, as did most of the others involved in the various theatrical performances. And I knew well enough to stay out of their way if I wanted to keep coming back to my hideaway.

On the afternoon of my mother's accident, my perch wasn't on a self-made sofa but on a folding director's chair in the corner by the rack of dresses. Each costume held a pungent fragrance of perfume, lotion, stage makeup, and perspiration. When they were all gathered together on the rack in a colorful assortment, the scent was exotic and strangely intoxicating. I knew that a bit of my mother's scent was mixed into that wild bouquet. So in my logically illogical preadolescent mind, I was somehow close to her.

I had settled in the director's chair reading *A Wrinkle in Time* and was at the part where the starfish grows back one of its appendages.

A panicked stagehand, dressed all in black, burst into the wardrobe and motioned for me to come with him. He said only three words: "It's your mother."

I read the truth in his face. I could see it all right there between the deeply creased lines radiating from his pinched eyes. She who had been to me all I knew of my past, present, and future was about to be severed from my life. I remember thinking in that micromoment that I would never be able to grow another Eve Carson the Actress to replace her.

As the train chugged on toward Carlton Heath, my tears came like quiet rain, remembering my mother and staring at the nativity scene on the box. Christmas was about birth, new life, and celebrating Christ. Last year all of that had been true. This year...I blew my nose and prayed that today would not be the day Ian would experience the severing of Andrew MacGregor from his life.

Chapter Four

Jan returned to his seat on the train carrying two insulated cups of hot tea. I knew he had been as far as he could get to the engine room, but I let him think I believed he had only been as far as the snack car.

"Twelve minutes," he said. "Twelve minutes before we arrive in Carlton Heath. My car is parked on the west end of the lot. We might have to put the top down to fit everything in. Is that your warmest coat?"

I nodded. It was the only coat I'd brought with me.

"The hospital is about ten kilometers from the station. Do you think you'll be warm enough?"

"I'll be fine. I have a scarf."

"Good." He sipped his tea. I could tell by his expression that it was too hot. Holding onto my cup, I waited for it to cool. A faintly cheering sense of familiarity came into view as I looked out the window and watched the red brick row houses with their slanted roofs and smoking chimney pots. I had looked forward to this day for so long. Never did I expect the ominous news that would run to meet us before we entered the village of Carlton Heath.

We didn't talk the rest of the way, but we did make good use of our nonverbal communication skills. Being in a long distance relationship for the past year, Ian and I had learned a variety of ways to communicate our affection, even though we were thousands of miles apart. On the train it felt like a luxury to squeeze his arm and offer him a comforting look. I knew he was taking in all my unspoken messages.

I'm not so sure he was able to read my unspoken messages once we arrived at the train station though. Ian smashed my small suitcase into the nearly nonexistent trunk of his Austin-Healy sports car, and I drew in a sharp breath through my closed teeth. He was in his "make it happen" mode for good reason. I was in the "save the presents" mode for equally good reason. I chose not to use that moment to communicate anything either verbally or nonverbally.

Drawing in the crisp winter air, I looked up at the clear sky and watched my breath form airy snowballs that instantly evaporated. This, I remembered. This moist, chilled air. This feeble covering of the ancient trees. This shade of pale blue above with hints of green and earthy brown below. The beauty of this small corner of England at this time of year was the beauty of lacy frost on the windows at first light and of long, willowy shadows at dusk.

Even in the midst of everything that was happening, I felt privileged to be here.

Crawling into the sports car on what still felt like it should be the driver's side, I buckled up before we took off for the hospital. I'd been with Ian before when he opened up on the country roads of Kent. We had gone for a picnic in the country last August when I was in England visiting him. I knew his "baby" could hum, and hum she did, all the way to the hospital. My ears froze, and my nose dripped from the cold, but my feet, tucked up under the heating vent, were nice and toasty.

Ian parked, pulled out my large suitcase, and quickly put the car's top in place. He took off for the hospital entrance with my suitcase bumping along over the uneven pavement of the parking lot.

As I trotted to keep up, a beautiful thought broke through my concern for Andrew and my growing exasperation with Ian. If I were the one lying in the hospital bed, Ian would race to my side just as he was racing to his father's side. Not since the loss of my mother did I have anyone in my life who would care and come for me in that way.

We found Andrew's room, and tall, graceful Katharine met us with hugs.

"How is he?" Ian marched past Katharine and went to his father's bedside.

"He's sedated," Katharine said in a soft voice. "The doctor should be around in a moment to talk with us about the test results." She reached for my hand and gave it a squeeze. "I'm so glad you're here, Miranda."

"I'm glad too." I squeezed her hand back.

"Dad, how are you feeling? Miranda and I are here now."

The sleeping giant only gave a twitch of his mouth in response, causing his snowy white beard to move slightly.

I slipped my hand into Andrew's where it rested on his

great, barreled chest. I couldn't imagine the world without this man.

You must heal, Andrew MacGregor. Do you hear me? Heal and mend. Get strong. You are so deeply loved by many. You can't leave us now. You can't. You have to stay with us.

"Are you comfortable, Dad? I can bring you another pillow if you like."

Andrew's only response was the steady rise and fall of his chest.

The doctor entered before Ian managed to extract a response from his father, which was probably a small kindness for the sedated man.

"What can you tell us?" Ian asked the doctor.

The doctor dove into an overview of what had happened to Andrew, what procedures had been followed, and how the test results had come back indicating no need for further concern.

"I have every reason to believe your father is going to pull through this. What he needs is lots of rest and some recommended adjustments to his diet and exercise. You'll receive the information when we release him."

"Does that mean he's able to go home now?" Ian asked.

"No, I'd like to keep him here for observation overnight to see how he responds to the medication I've started him on. If he has no adverse reactions, I'll provide you with that prescription. He's a strong man, and I anticipate a full recovery."

"What a relief," I said softly.

"Have you any further questions for me?" the doctor asked.

Ian glanced at Katharine and me and then back at the doctor. "No. This is better news than we had hoped for. Keep on giving him your best care. That's all I ask."

"That is the plan, Mr. MacGregor," he said.

I knew Ian would like his answer. Ian liked having a plan.

The doctor left, and Ian pressed his chin against the top of my head, kissing me on the crown. "This is good news," he said. "Very good news. If you need to go for a bit, Katharine, I'll look after things here."

"Well," Katharine lowered herself into the chair next to the bed and said, "I was planning to stay. But since you're here, I should check in at the Tea Cosy. I left Ellie in charge of serving the expected holiday guests, and it is close to teatime."

"What about the Christmas play tonight?" I asked.

For the past forty years the Carlton Heath Theatre Guild had carried on a tradition of performing Charles Dickens's *A Christmas Carol* at Grey Hall. I knew this was the first year the Guild had an all-children cast—except for Andrew. He was playing the showstopper role of Father Christmas.

I remembered going to the production last Christmas Eve and watching Andrew take on the role of Christmas Present. Before Andrew created his own adaptation of the Father Christmas character in the Christmas Present scene, the part had belonged to my father.

Ellie, my half brother's wife, had told me many stories of how Sir James Whitcombe took to the stage each year and embodied the role. He was Father Christmas to all the children in the village of Carlton Heath. He visited their homes and schools with gifts and good cheer, and when he passed away, the town mourned the loss longer than any of his devoted fans with their blogs and Web sites.

In some ways the town still was mourning. This year was

only their third Christmas without Sir James. Andrew had given the role a worthy run, but now he was unable to don the hooded Father Christmas costume and bring hope and cheer to the stage and to the people of Carlton Heath.

"I'm waiting to hear from the Guild director," Katharine said. "He is considering postponing tonight's performance in light of Andrew's situation. If they do postpone, we'll have a performance on Christmas Eve. We hadn't planned on that since we felt the children should be home on the night before Christmas."

"Do you think Andrew will be well enough to resume his role by tomorrow night?" I asked optimistically.

A low rumble sounded from Andrew's chest. "I'm not dead yet. Or had none of you noticed that?"

"There he is!" Ian leaned over his father. "Ready to give out orders again, are you?"

Ian looked at me and smiled. The room seemed to have suddenly become more spacious.

"What have they done to me, son?" Andrew's eyelids fluttered open and then closed again.

"You had a mild heart attack, Dad."

"Feels more like a Saxon attack."

The three of us smiled.

"What day is it?" Andrew asked, still not opening his eyes.

"It's December twenty-third." I slipped my hand into Andrew's large paw.

"And whose soft hand is this?"

"It's Miranda's, Dad. We're all here for you."

"Where's my Katharine?"

"I'm right here." Katharine rose and kissed his forehead. "You're on the mend, Andrew. The doctor said we're not to worry. You need to rest now."

"How can a man be expected to sleep when he's flanked by his son and two beautiful women?" Andrew's closed eyelids fluttered as if they were just too heavy to open. A smooth expression came over his rugged face. The three of us watched as his mouth drooped, and his breathing returned to the steady rhythm of sleep.

"Go on, then," Ian whispered to Katharine. "I'll stay with him. I'm sure he's going to be sleeping for the next while."

Katharine nodded, as if she finally agreed leaving might be the best choice. Turning to me she said, "Is there a chance you might want to come with me?"

"Sure. Do you need some help?"

"I wouldn't mind some. I left everything in such shambles."

"Of course. I can go to the Tea Cosy with you now, if that would help."

"Yes, that would be best. Ian, are you all right with that plan?"

"Yes. I can manage here. Miranda, don't make any commitments for dinner though. Particularly with men in ski caps." He gave me a wink. "I'll meet you at the Cosy at seven o'clock sharp."

"I'll be ready," I said.

"And I'll be ready too," Andrew mumbled without opening his eyes.

"No, you'll be sleeping, Dad, if you know what's good for you."

"Being with all of you, that's what's good for me. That and maybe a kiss or two."

Andrew rumbled right into a slurred and paraphrased version of a poem I'd heard him quote a number of times. The name of the kiss-giver seemed to change according to whom he was trying to coerce at the moment. This afternoon it was me.

"Say I'm weary, say I'm sad;

"Say that health and wealth have missed me;

"Say I'm growing old, but add—

"Miranda kissed me!"

In response, I planted a nice, warm kiss on his whiskered cheek and whispered my own paraphrased version of one of my favorite quotes from Shakespeare's *Much Ado About Nothing*. I had many lines memorized from my mother's performances, which I heard over and over. "Serve God, love well, and mend."

Chapter Five

*a*re you sure you're not too tired to do this?" Katharine asked once we were in her car and on our way back into town.

She had a good point. Usually this was when my jet lag kicked in. "No, I'm wide awake. I think the scare with Andrew had something to do with that. All that adrenaline."

"Che-che-che," Katharine responded in soothing agreement. The funny sound she made reminded me of the indistinct call a person made to attract a squirrel or a flock of birds. During the past year her "che-che-che" had come to mean many things to me, including the sense of comfort she was bestowing on both of us now.

That's how it was with Katharine. Her husband had just suffered a heart attack, and yet she was asking about me, making sure I wasn't too tired. I loved Katharine. I loved Andrew, and without a doubt I loved Ian. I was more than ready for our everyday lives to intersect the way they were now. But a few items needed to be resolved to pull all the pieces together. My hopes for this trip included settling those issues.

Just as my thoughts went to one of those unresolved concerns, Katharine inadvertently brought up the topic. "I thought you should know that Margaret plans to come to the Tea Cosy this afternoon."

Katharine turned off the main road and took the shortcut to Bexley Lane where her tea shop was located.

"Oh good," I said. But I could tell my enthusiasm level wasn't convincing by the look on Katharine's face as she glanced at me.

Unlike my mother, I couldn't act well. I could pretend, however. And ever since I had entered the scene with the Whitcombe family here in Carlton Heath, I had pretended that Margaret would one day accept me. She didn't have to like me, but I imagined all sorts of ways she could receive me into the clan.

Margaret was the matriarch of the Whitcombe family now that my father was dead. She was my father's only wife. Understandably, my sudden appearance along with the evidence I produced to verify my place in the Whitcombe lineage was distressing to her, which is why I had done everything I could to keep my identity quiet.

This was a small village. The Whitcombes and MacGregors were close friends. As much as I wanted the awkwardness to magically go away between all of us, I knew it would probably be like this for a long time.

Even so, I liked to imagine all would be well. Ian and I would marry. We would move to Carlton Heath. Margaret would accept me, and I would at long last be "home." I would finally belong somewhere. And I would be part of a family.

Katharine was halfway down the bumpy, narrow back road that I called the "romantic route" because it went past the ivy-covered church with the old cemetery, the magnificent trees with their gnarled trunks, and a collection of stone cottages with trimmed hedges. One of the cottages held a special memory for me, and I was eager to see it again.

Katharine came upon what I had dubbed "Forgotten Rose Cottage" because of the surplus of neglected rosebushes that grew up both sides of the stone dwelling. She slowed the car and veered around a pothole.

"I love that little place," I said.

"Lovely, isn't it?" Katharine offered me a soft smile.

The long-neglected stone cottage looked different than it had last summer. Someone had done a significant amount of cleanup.

"Did someone buy the cottage?"

"It's possible."

My heart sank. I had dreams about that little, fairy-tale house. I dreamed of one day acquiring the place with Ian. I could see us working side by side in our jeans and sweatshirts, painting and decorating and making the long-neglected cottage into a home. Our home.

But that would never be if someone else had snatched up the Forgotten Rose Cottage and decided to make it their dream.

A chest-tightening sadness came over me, and I felt an urge to fight for the house. "Is there a way to find out if someone has bought it?"

"I'm sure there is. You should ask Ian. He has ways of finding out such things quickly."

I crossed my arms in front of me and thought of the many things Ian and I needed to discuss this week. Maybe I should have stayed at the hospital with him instead of stepping right into seeing Margaret my first few hours in Carlton Heath.

Glancing at Katharine, I realized I'd been so wrapped up in my own world that I hadn't asked how she was doing with the fright of Andrew and his trip to the hospital. For the rest of the short drive to the Tea Cosy, I put my attention on Katharine.

And in her Katharine way, she put twice as much love and attention right back on me.

As she turned her car onto Bexley Lane, the long awaited sight didn't disappoint. Every lamppost on this beautiful stretch of road was adorned with a large evergreen wreath. Long garlands of evergreen and ivy dotted with red berries hung from one lamppost to the next. The wreaths as well as the swaying garlands were trimmed in twinkling lights and pert, red ribbons.

Even though it was only dusk, all the lights were lit, turning this street into a twinkling fairyland that looked like a Victorian Christmas card. Of all the places of business on Bexley Lane, the Tea Cosy exuded the most charm. The building was one of the oldest in Carlton Heath; made of rock and limestone, it hinted at being a well-aged, diminutive castle. The sign that hung on the lamppost adjacent to the shop was in the shape of a teapot.

As Katharine and I approached the front door, I stepped ahead of her just for the personal delight of being the one to reach for the oddly-shaped metal latch and to open the heavy, wooden door. The string of merry silver bells jumped and jingled, and once again I stepped over the timber threshold and entered one of my favorite places in the world, the Tea Cosy.

A warm, amber fire burned in the ancient hearth of the permanently soot-covered fireplace. Along the mantel and at each table small red votive candles flickered contentedly.

I took a quick look around and spotted Margaret. She was seated in the far corner in a tall chair with her back to the door.

"Shall we?" Katharine asked.

I knew she was asking if we should go and greet Margaret. With a nod, I followed Katharine across the uneven wooden floor. She spoke in her buttery smooth way. "Hallo, Margaret. We've good news on Andrew. Did you hear?"

"No. Only that he had gone to hospital. How is he?" With a sideways glance at me, Margaret added, "Welcome back, Miranda."

She was a round and rosy woman with fair skin, white hair, and wire-rimmed glasses. Not the sort of looks one imagines for the wife of such a distinguished film star, but Margaret carried herself with a regal air.

"It's good to be back." I reached for Margaret in preparation to greet her with a hug or at least a handshake. When she didn't respond in kind, I ended up giving her arm an awkward pat.

Ellie, my half brother's petite, sparkling wife, must have heard Katharine and me because she flitted out of the kitchen in her white apron with a tray of warm scones in her hands. On her head perched a headband with felt reindeer antlers.

Ellie loved life. She loved people. As soon as she saw me, she put the scones on the table for Margaret and threw her arms around me in a welcoming hug.

"You're here! This is perfect. Julia has been counting the days until her Auntie Miranda arrives. She's at the house, hoping you'll go there first. I suppose you've been to hospital, though, isn't that right? How is Andrew? We've all been so concerned, haven't we?"

"Yes," Margaret said. "What is the news of Andrew?"

Katharine gave the good report and added, "We don't anticipate any complications or further problems. It's the best report we could have received, really."

Ellie clapped her hands together. "Wonderful news!"

"I'm so pleased to hear such a report," Margaret said. "What a relief that must be for all of you."

"Yes, it's a blessed relief. Miranda and I have come back to do some baking that went by the wayside this morning. Before I get everything ready in the kitchen, would you care for more tea?"

"Yes, that would be lovely. Miranda, would you care to join me?"

I looked at Katharine and back at Margaret. Had I been set up for this meeting? I didn't think so. Arranging this meeting would have been a challenge, given all the details that hadn't gone according to schedule so far that day.

"If you don't mind, Katharine," Ellie said, untying the strings on her apron, "I must go on a quick errand. Your timing is perfect, really. I need to make a dash."

"Of course. I appreciate all you did today."

"It was a pleasure." Reaching for my arm as I lowered myself into the chair across from Margaret, Ellie said, "I'll see you back here in less than an hour."

"I'll be here."

As Katharine and Ellie left me alone at the table with Margaret, I noted that I had the same feeling I'd experienced on my first job interview. As much as I wanted Margaret to accept me, I still didn't like sitting there, not knowing what the outcome of our meeting was going to be.

"How fortunate that you and I have this opportunity to speak with each other privately before the holiday festivities begin," Margaret said.

I nodded, waiting.

"I have wanted to tell you how much I have appreciated your discretion this past year. Edward and I were speaking not long ago of the unique situation between you and our family. Edward reminded me of how you are to be commended for your maturity and prudence." Margaret paused as if waiting for my response.

The only words that came to mind were, "Thank you."

Margaret seemed like the sort of woman who did a lot of thinking on a subject before letting her opinions be known. I couldn't tell if she had expressed all that was on her mind. A weighted "however" statement seemed as if it might follow, and I waited for it in bone-dry silence.

But apparently Margaret had said all she intended to. At least at this point.

She reached for her china teacup and took a small sip. I leaned back and felt as if the adrenaline-delayed jet lag had come over me all at once.

"I should probably see if I can help Katharine with the tea," I said.

"Yes, of course."

Feeling officially dismissed, I got up and was almost to the curtain that separated the small kitchen from the dining area when the sound of the cheery jingle bells on the front door announced that someone else had entered.

I turned to see who it was, and for the second time that day I saw the last person I expected.

Chapter Six

"How about that?" Josh sported a victorious grin as soon as he saw me. "The guy at the train station said this might be the place."

All eyes were on Josh as he dropped his heavy bag off his shoulder and bumped the chair of one of the guests closest to the door.

"Oh, sorry. Pardon me." He nodded at the ruffled woman. She raised her gaze to his ski cap, and he immediately removed it. Unfortunately, his uncombed and most likely unwashed hair looked worse than the ski beanie.

I tried to direct him back, preferably out the door, but at least away from the guests. So far, on all my visits to Carlton Heath, none of the busybodies seemed to find my connection to their town or to the Whitcombes or MacGregors out of the ordinary. That was because Ian and I were such an item of interest. I was sure our names had been discussed more than once over the chubby china teapots positioned between the ladies who loved to gather at the Tea Cosy for a good chat.

This scene with Josh was guaranteed to be a teatime tale for many weeks if I didn't find a way to redirect this inconvenient American out the door and on his way.

I tried to make it appear as if I were simply addressing a wayward tourist and not someone I knew when I said in a low voice, "I'm not sure this is where you want to be right now."

"Why? Is a private party going on here?" Josh wasn't catching any of my subtle hints, conveyed through a variety of facial expressions.

"No, but…"

"Then would it be okay if I ordered something to eat?"

I knew how determined Josh could be once he put his mind to something. If he wasn't going to leave, the path of least disruption would be to tuck him into a corner and try to keep him quiet. At least until most of the curious women went on their way.

Putting on my hostess demeanor, I said, "Go ahead and take a seat. I'll bring you some tea."

I started to head for the kitchen when out of the corner of my eye I saw that Josh was making a beeline for an empty table in the far back corner—the table next to Margaret's.

"Actually," I said quickly intervening, "I think you would be better off at the table over here by the kitchen. There is more room for your baggage."

Boy, was that an understatement. If there were any way I could tuck him *inside* the kitchen, then our mutual baggage would be less obvious to everyone. *This is not good. I wish I'd insisted he leave instead of making a place for him.*

Ducking into the tiny kitchen and pulling the curtain shut behind me, I closed my eyes and tried to think. I could feel myself panting.

"What is it?" Katharine asked.

I put my finger to my lips, hopeful that nothing we said could be heard beyond the curtain. Yet I knew all too well how easily sound carried in this place.

In a low whisper, I pointed to the other side of the wall. "My old boyfriend! I ran into him at the train station in London. I told him about Carlton Heath. I never thought he would come here!"

Katharine, in her serene way, handed me a pot of fresh tea. "Please tell our guest the scones will be ready shortly."

If I hadn't counted Katharine as a close friend as well as my (hopefully) soon-to-be mother-in-law, I would have protested.

Exiting the kitchen with the pot of tea in one hand and a china cup and saucer in the other, I was aware that every eye in the room was on Josh. Some of the women stared from adjusted positions and postures that weren't exactly covert. Flora, who owned the Bexley Lane Gifts and Curios Shoppe, had been preparing to leave her table at the Tea Cosy when I first arrived.

She now had joined another table, and all three women had positioned their chairs so they faced the kitchen. As soon as I entered the dining area, I felt the curious gazes shift from Josh to their tea and scones, as if I were a teacher who had stepped out in the middle of an exam and returned before the naughty students had finished copying each other's answers.

Katharine followed me out of the kitchen and took another fresh pot of tea to Margaret. I appreciated her going to Margaret. Katharine would know what to say.

As I placed the tea and cup in front of Josh, he said in a low voice, "Hey, I just realized this might be awkward for you."

I was sure he caught onto that brilliant insight as soon as he noticed the attention he was receiving from the curious audience.

"It could be awkward for you, as well," I whispered.

"Is there someplace else we can go? Just for a few minutes?"

I shook my head. "This is a very small village."

"So it seems. It's great, though, isn't it? Bexley Lane, just like the address printed on the back of the photo. I had no problem finding my way here. I can see why you like it so much."

"Josh, is there a reason you came here?" I knew if we kept our voices low, we might not be heard. This table by the kitchen was the most isolated, which is why few guests ever chose to sit there. It also helped if I stood because the way the table was angled, my back would block Josh from his audience.

"I came because I was curious to see this place. My flight was overbooked, so when free tickets were offered in exchange for seats, I was the first one at the counter. My rescheduled flight goes out at midnight, and I thought, 'Who knows when I'll be in England again? Why not go to Carlton Heath?' And here I am."

"But how did you know you would find me here at the Tea Cosy?"

"That was easy. When I described you to the guy at the train station, he said you had gone off with someone named Ian in his Austin-Healy. He said Ian is related to the owner of this place."

I felt myself relaxing slightly. His explanations made sense.

This was his idea of a diversion. A little adventure. He would drink a cup of tea, leave, and tell all his associates about his train ride to the English countryside between his flights.

I poured the first cup of tea for him in an effort to appear to have a reason for lingering at his table.

Josh smiled up at me. And that's when I knew I was in trouble. It was his flirty, how-you-doin' smile, not his good-to-see-you-but-I-gotta-go smile.

"So, I have a question for you," he said, trying to come across casually. I could tell he was nervous though.

"What's your question?"

He cleared his throat. "I realize I'm putting myself way out there, but after seeing you at Paddington station, I had to ask. Are you with anyone now?"

"Yes, I am with someone."

Josh seemed to slump in his chair. "I thought that's what you might say. By any chance, is it the guy with the Austin-Healy?"

I nodded.

"Well, at least I can say he has good taste in cars and women."

I tried to offer a friendly, consolation prize sort of smile, but one thing puzzled me.

In my lowest of low voices, I asked, "Did I give you any signal, any indication at all, at the train station that I was available?"

"No." Josh shook his head. "You just look amazing and I was... well, a guy can hope, can't he?"

I knew all about hoping. For the past year I'd begun to hope about many things, including the fanciful wish that I might one day live in the Forgotten Rose Cottage, even though no indication had ever been given to me that it might be available. That small flit of a thought gave me enough compassion to excuse Josh's impulsive decision to seek me out. He was, after all, one of the few people in my life with whom I'd had a close relationship at one time.

"Listen." Josh aligned himself so that my standing position more thoroughly blocked him from the ladies. I was sure by now the ones with hearing aids had their devices turned up all the way.

"There is one more thing I wanted to say to you. Do you remember my brother?"

I nodded.

"He's a lawyer now, and I thought you should know, in case you need representation for..."

I gave Josh a determined look that fortunately silenced him. I knew where he was going. If I was the daughter of Sir James, certainly someone needed to assist me in fighting for my rightful portion of his inheritance. I'd been over this road already, and my choice had been to let it go. I never went in search of my birth father with the anticipation of financial gain. All I wanted was information and hopefully a relationship. I had received what I went after. I never wanted to jeopardize my fledgling family relationships by going up against Edward or Margaret with a claim to anything. End of discussion.

"I take it you have all that covered," he said, reading my not-so-subliminal message.

"Yes. It's covered. And I want to tell you again how glad I am that you regard information with complete confidentiality. As a professional, I mean."

"Got it." He obviously understood my masked message that I was counting on him to keep silent about my identity.

Leaning back and looking at the cup of tea in front of him, he said, "So, I guess I should try some of this English tea before I leave."

"Yes, you should." I was referring to the "should leave" part more than the "try the tea" part. But at the same time, I knew I would never forget my first visit to the Tea Cosy and my first pot of proper British tea and plate of Katharine's scones. I did want him to enjoy the fruit of his adventurous trek from Heathrow.

"I need to get back to the kitchen," I said.

"I understand. Really, I do."

I could tell Josh was now the one sending the cryptic message. He never had been one to overstay his welcome.

"You seem to fit in here," he said almost as an afterthought. "But, you know, if things don't work out with...whatever, you know how to contact me."

In an effort to keep our parting light and breezy and as uncomplicated as possible, I said, "Well, you know, if that counseling practice of yours doesn't work out, you can always try detective work."

Josh smiled.

"I'll see about the scones to go with your tea."

As if we were a well-orchestrated team, Katharine came up next to me just then and offered Josh a plate of warm scones along with clotted cream and jam. She explained how to open the scone and spread the jam first, leaving the clotted cream for the dollop on top. While she extended her hospitality, I headed back into the kitchen.

With a quick glance to the back of the room, I saw Margaret directing a quick glance our way.

Whatever your perception is about all this, Margaret, please don't jump to any conclusions. I don't care what the other women here think. I do care immensely, though, about what you think.

Chapter Seven

From the kitchen, I could hear everything being said as it seeped through the curtain. Flora apparently had decided to take her leave but found it necessary to shuffle over to Josh's table to greet Katharine before making her departure.

After exchanging pleasantries about how Andrew was improving in hospital, Flora spoke to Josh in a timbre loud enough for most of the room to hear. "I do hope you're enjoying your tea and scones. We're all quite fond of Katharine's baking here. A little too fond, some of us are, I should think."

"I can see why you'd feel that way," Josh said in what I recognized to be his counselor sort of response.

"It's not often that we see visitors in our little village. We're not exactly a tourist destination, are we?"

"It's a charming place," Josh said politely.

"Our resident royalty seemed to think so," a second woman's voice chimed in. "One of the charms of Carlton Heath, of course, is the quiet. At least that's how things have been since his passing."

"She means Sir James, of course," Flora added.

"I see." Again, Josh seemed to be using his counselor responses to keep engaged in the conversation, yet remain aloof and noncommittal as to how much he actually knew.

I realized at that moment that Josh's expert "engaged yet noncommittal" demeanor had been a hallmark of our relationship. Even though we connected on a number of levels while we dated, we never had melded at the heart level the way Ian and I had almost instantly. My relationship with Margaret as well as with my half brother, Edward, bore the same characteristics as my relationship with Josh. We were connected or "engaged," as it were, in many areas. Yet aloofness was what marked the relationship.

Since Josh didn't seem to be snapping at any of the bait thrown into the conversation about Carlton Heath's most famous resident, Flora tried once more with a subdued announcement that Sir James's widow was in their presence. "She's the one in the corner there. A lovely woman, really. Rather given to her own company though. Not that anyone could blame her. We all understand why, don't we? After living in her husband's shadow all those years, the dear has spent most of her time trying to stay out of the limelight. She's become rather accomplished at being amongst us yet staying invisible, if you will."

My heart suddenly went out to Margaret. She and I were more alike than I had ever thought. I, too, was acquainted with the art of making myself invisible. I knew all too well the loneliness that incubated in such places as backstage wardrobe rooms and back tables in busy tea shops.

"I'm rather curious," Flora said. "If you don't mind my asking, what does one manage to cart around in such a large duffel bag?"

Josh's mumbled response must have been meant to be heard only by Flora because I couldn't make out what he said.

Flora certainly heard his answer. Her "Oh my!" response echoed off the kitchen walls. I could hear a faint twittering throughout the Cosy, as if each of the observers was checking with the others to see if anyone had heard what he said.

The bells on the door jingled, suggesting that Flora was making a hasty exit. Katharine appeared in the kitchen with her cheeks rosy and her lips upturned.

"What did he say to her?" I whispered.

Katharine cupped her hand to my ear. "He told her his duffel bag was large enough to carry his dead aunt."

Covering my mouth, I muffled my laugh. I'd forgotten all about Josh's morose sense of humor. I knew he *really* needed to get out of town now.

The diversion he had just created was a gift to me, whether he meant it as such or not. The topic of the day would now be about Josh and the speculations on his poor auntie instead of whether he and I were somehow connected. I owed him for that one.

Rummaging in my purse for a slip of paper, I wrote Josh a quick note.

Thank you! I hope all goes well for you.
(And your unfortunate auntie!)

Returning to the dining area, I planned to slip him the note as if it were the bill, even though I knew Katharine wouldn't charge him since he was a special guest.

When I stepped past the curtain, nearly everyone was already gone, including Josh. Margaret was gone as well. It didn't surprise me that a number of the women had ducked out, no doubt with the objective of bustling to the nearest phone to start the alert.

I could picture Josh trekking to the train station down Bexley Lane with his duffel bag over his shoulder. A number of certain residents between here and the station would be, at this very moment, answering their hotly ringing phones and hurrying to their windows to have a look as he passed by.

With all the excitement over, a friendly calm returned to the Cosy. I put more wood on the fire, cleared the tables, and went to work washing dishes. Last August I'd helped out here one afternoon while Katharine went for a hair appointment and Ian and Andrew repaired the plumbing in the apartment upstairs. Even though the building was old, Andrew had managed to do an impressive job of updating the four-room apartment space where he and Katharine lived.

I experienced a calming and unexpected contentment last August while carrying out the simple domestic tasks that accompanied the running of a tea shop. When Katharine returned from her hair appointment, I told her I preferred the work I'd put my hands to that afternoon over the tedious work I'd done at a large accounting firm in San Francisco for almost ten years.

When I tried to explain to Katharine that this was a place of peace for me, she said, "You are a woman drawn to home and hearth. Never doubt the happiness such simplicity can bring you."

From that moment, I knew I had a place here. It was as if my internal compass had reset and would now always point to the Tea Cosy and to Katharine, the woman who filled this small space with so much love and grace.

The timer on the stove gave a dull buzz. I put on an oven mitt and pulled out two trays of Katharine's warm, fragrant shortbread Christmas cookies. I'd tasted these cookies on previous visits, and the sight and scent of them started my mouth watering. Katharine called these cookies "Andrew's Scottish shortbread biscuits" and had confided to me that her secret ingredient was Madagascar vanilla bean.

Usually Katharine used a round cookie cutter on the thickly rolled-out dough. This time the cookies cooling on the trays were cut in the shape of stars. Christmas stars.

I looked at the plumped-up stars and once again thought of the imagery of the five-armed starfish from *A Wrinkle in Time* and how it related to the loss of my mother. She was the missing part of me, the part that had so defined who I was and what I would become.

Reaching for a spatula, I slipped it under one of the Christmas star cookies and lifted it so I could touch the warm star, my finger gently tapping on each of the five appendages.

Just then Katharine entered the kitchen. I looked up at her, and I knew. I just knew. The broken star of my life had been made whole through the gift of her friendship. The part I thought I would go through life without had grown back when I wasn't watching.

Chapter Eight

Sometimes when revelations come, they must be spoken aloud to become fully vested. Those breakthrough moments of understanding, accepting, and receiving are validated and affirmed in the presence of another.

That had been the case for me last Christmas when I sensed a constant, gentle presence throughout my time in Carlton Heath. At the church where I sat beside Ellie on Christmas morning, studying the Christ figure portrayed in the stained glass windows, I was compelled to believe in God.

I didn't know it at the time, but two things were happening at once. As I was trying to find a way to enter into what I knew would be a life-changing conversation with Edward and Margaret, God's Spirit seemed to be closing in on me with the same objective. On the one hand, I wanted to reveal to the Whitcombes that, because of Sir James, I was related to them by blood. On the other hand, God was trying to reveal to me that because of His Son and because of His blood, I could enter God's family.

I still don't know how to describe what happened that day in such a simple, quiet way except to say that I believed. I went from not belonging to God and His kingdom to being accepted and belonging to Him and His eternal family. I understood that my connection to Him came because of Christ's blood. It was that simple and that impossibly complex all at the same time.

With Edward and Margaret, it seemed to be still mostly complex. I was related to them—or at least to Edward—by blood. Yet I still was waiting to be fully accepted into their family.

Last Christmas Katharine had been the first one to whom I had entrusted the story of what seemed to me mysterious, ancient, and true. The story of how I had been pursued by God, and now I was changed. I belonged to Christ.

When I spoke my revelation to her, the truth was sealed. I was a believer of infantile status, but a Christian nonetheless. I was a fledgling follower of Christ, and I knew she was someone who had followed close to Him for many years.

The foundation of our friendship began to grow that day, I think. And now, a year later, as I held the Christmas star cookie in my hand, I saw what had grown in my life where for a long time all that had existed was great loss.

I put down the cookie and stepped over to Katharine in that small kitchen space. Wrapping my arms around her, I whispered in her ear, "I love you."

"I love you too, Miranda." She stroked my hair and released a breathy "che-che-che" sound, as if she were calming a small bird.

Aside from my mother and Ian, Katharine was the only

other person on this planet to whom I had said, "I love you." I think she knew that.

We pulled apart. Not awkwardly, but like two dancers. I hadn't hugged Katharine exactly like that before, but it instantly felt like a familiar motion, as if we were well acquainted with the ways of all close mothers and daughters.

She smiled at me and spoke a single word filled with hope. "Soon."

I nodded. I knew what she meant. Ian took Katharine into his confidences as well. I'm sure she knew about the small box he had picked up that morning in London. She undoubtedly knew what was in the box. And she was probably feeling a similar anticipation, waiting for what we both knew would be one of Ian's well-planned moments when the box was opened.

Katharine slid two more cookie sheets of shortbread into the oven, and the two of us went about the kitchen duties as if this were the next act in the ancient, domestic ballet of women.

We had nearly finished all the cleanup from the afternoon teatime when the jolly jingle bells let us know someone else had entered the Cosy. We didn't need to step out of the kitchen to see who it was. The merry voices let us know right away that Ellie had returned with her observant thirteen-year-old son, Mark, and precocious six-year-old daughter, Julia.

"Auntie Miranda!" Julia sang out her greeting. "Auntie Katharine! Where are you?"

"In the kitchen," Katharine called out in a matching, sing-song voice.

Brown-haired Julia burst through the curtain and entered the kitchen with a squeal. She wrapped her arms around my middle and hug, hug, hugged me.

"How's my favorite little girl?" I asked, kissing the top of her head.

"Your favorite little girl is happy you are finally here! Have you seen it yet?"

"Have I seen what?"

Katharine intervened. "Julia, it's not yet Christmas. We have to keep a few things secret until then."

Julia placed both hands over her mouth, and I gave Katharine a raised eyebrow look. Katharine, the one who didn't make it a practice to keep secrets, was directing young Julia to do just that. Well, well, well!

Peeking around my middle, Julia eyed the cookies. "Are those biscuits for anyone special?"

"Julia!" Ellie spouted, entering the kitchen and catching her little beggar in the act.

Julia turned her innocent eyes to Katharine, and a Christmas star was in her hand before Ellie had another opportunity to protest.

"Only one," Ellie said. "And see if your brother would like one as well."

"Markie!"

"Please don't screech like that, Julia. Go ask your brother politely and in an inside voice," Ellie said.

"Here." Katharine handed over another biscuit. "I have a feeling his answer will be yes."

Julia trotted out with a plump star in each hand.

"Have you heard the news about tonight's performance?" Ellie asked.

"We understood the Guild was considering canceling," I said.

"Not so," Ellie said gleefully. "The Theatre Guild has decided not to cancel the performance tonight. The curtain will go up as scheduled, and guess who will be donning the robes of Father Christmas?"

"Certainly not Andrew," Katharine said.

"No, not Andrew. Have you another guess?"

Neither Katharine nor I could come up with an obvious choice. Ellie's husband, Edward, would be the next logical Father Christmas since he was Sir James's son and therefore would be immediately received by the townspeople since Andrew wasn't available. However, Edward wasn't the sort to ever appear onstage. He stayed far away from his father's footsteps. In this regard, he and I shared a common goal.

"I will give you a hint," Ellie said. "We were just at Grey Hall and saw the new Father Christmas having a costume fitting, and Mavis was telling him he was quite a catch. But he told her he already was taken."

"Ian?" Katharine and I said in unison.

"Ohh. Did I give too much of a clue?" Ellie looked disappointed at our deductions. Had she forgotten what a small village this was?

Just then my cell phone rang with the customized tune that told me Ian was calling. "Speaking of the jolly ole elf..."

"Ho, ho, ho," I answered.

"Madam, you seem to have mistaken me for my American counterpart."

"Then should I have said, 'Hee, hee, hee?' I heard the news."

"So you did. Ellie is there now, I take it?"

"Yes, she's here with the kids. How's your dad?"

"Much improved and sleeping soundly. Listen, you and I will have to reschedule our dinner plans."

"Well, that's a good thing because it just so happens I have a play to attend tonight. I'm hoping to get a good seat right up front."

"I'll be looking for you there. How is Mark?"

"Fine, I guess. I haven't seen him yet. Why?"

"He'll be onstage tonight as well."

I knew Mark was an understudy for Scrooge in this all-children performance of Dickens's classic play. Apparently Andrew wasn't the only one who wasn't well enough to carry on that evening.

As soon as Ian and I said our "see you laters," I left Ellie and Katharine and went to check on Mark. The two women had stepped up the biscuit production now that the treats were definitely needed for that evening's refreshment table at intermission.

I found Mark seated beside the hearth about to make the last bite of cookie disappear. Julia was pretending she was the tearoom hostess, flitting from table to table with an imaginary pot of tea and chattering with her invisible friends.

Mark greeted me politely, and I pulled up a chair next to him by the waning fire. "I heard you have the leading role tonight."

"Yes, I do." His thin lips pulled tight in a squiggly line. Bits of shortbread crumbs dotted the corners.

"You're going to do a great job. I'm just sure of it."

Mark didn't look convinced, but he thanked me all the same.

"Are you feeling nervous?"

He shrugged bravely.

"I'll tell you a little trick that might help. My mother used to tell herself every opening night that it was only a dress rehearsal. She said she never got the jitters."

"Was your mother in a lot of performances?"

"Yes, she was."

"Did she go to a lot of parties?"

"A lot of parties? I don't know. I suppose she went to some. She went to cast parties with the other actors."

"What did they do at those parties?"

"Same sort of things you do at the cast parties here. Eat and talk about the performance."

Mark reached for the iron poker and taunted the roasted logs into bursting into what looked like a thousand escaping fireflies. He seemed to be pondering my answer rather intensely.

"Did that answer your question, Mark?"

"Sort of."

"What is it you wanted to know?"

"I wanted to know..." he hesitated, breaking the depleted log in half by hitting it directly in its hollowed center.

"What?" I wanted him to know he had my full attention.

"Did your mother kiss a lot of men?"

I drew back and tried to read Mark's expression. "Why did you ask that?"

Mark shrugged.

I didn't leave his comment alone. "What prompted you to ask that question?"

Mark looked down at his feet. "It's because I know."

"Because you know what?"

Without looking up he said in a low voice, "I know who your father was."

Chapter Nine

let out a slow, steady breath. "Did someone tell you about my mother, Mark?"

"No. No one told me. I heard my grandmother talking to my father. The parts they didn't say, I figured out."

I thought a moment. "Have you told anyone what you heard?"

"No." He adamantly shook his head.

"I think you should tell your parents and your grandmother. They would like to know what you heard."

"But I wasn't trying to listen in on them."

"I know. But since you did hear them talking, I think you should tell them what you heard."

"Is it true then?"

For a moment I considered dodging the question. I knew I could think of a way to avoid telling Mark the truth. That's what my mother did. She spun many fanciful tales in response to my challenging questions and managed to effortlessly enchant me right out of reality and into the realm where I could pretend that life was something other than what it was. For a moment I wondered if that was the best approach to take with Mark.

Then I thought of Katharine and her penchant for not hiding truth once it was revealed. Even Josh the psychologist, with his comments on how truth always rises to the surface, would tell me to be honest with Mark. What was it Josh had said about how sometimes you must wait for truth to surface and other times you must go to it, take it by the hand, and pull with all your might?

Mark had bravely taken truth by the hand and now was pulling with all his might. He could end up carrying my response with him the rest of his life.

I reached over and put my hand on Mark's shoulder. "Yes, it's true. My father was Sir James."

Mark didn't reply. In the hardening lines around his eyes, I instantly saw the reason my mother told fairytales instead of truths. Her lies were a misplaced sort of kindness, I suppose, in that it was her way of protecting my sensitive, young spirit. Perhaps my quirky mother and the bohemian lifestyle she imposed on me was her attempt to do the best she could with what she had. Don't all mothers do that? What my mother had was a wealth of fantasy.

Mark's dark hair fell across his forehead as he looked down at his hands. "Why do you think she did it?" he asked in a low voice.

I wasn't sure what he meant, so I asked him to expand his question.

"Why do you think your mother...you know...did what she did with my grandfather?"

I had no immediate response for him.

"I know how babies are born," Mark said with a muffled fierceness. "You don't need to pretend I don't know anything like Julia." Backing down he added, "If I shouldn't be asking this sort of question, then..."

"No, it's okay. The answer is, I don't know. I think my mother loved your grandfather. I really do. I think they probably both felt something meaningful and real toward each other when they met. Your grandparents were separated at the time..."

"I know," Mark said quickly.

"So when your grandparents got back together, my mother chose not to tell him she was expecting me. She raised me by herself, and we just went on."

An airy stretch of silence fashioned invisible bonds between my astute nephew and me. I reached over and gave his hand a small squeeze. His fingers were cold. He looked up with a softened expression that reminded me of Ellie. He definitely had his father's sharp, analytical mind, but he also had his mother's tender spirit toward all living creatures.

"Thanks for talking to me about it," he said in an adult-sounding voice.

"You're welcome."

His wobbly, thin-line smile returned: "Whenever I call you Aunt Miranda, everyone else will think it's still because you're a family friend. But I'll know who you really are."

I leaned over and pressed a motherly kiss on the side of his head. In a whisper I said, "And I will always know who you are, Mark Whitcombe. You are my amazing nephew. And I will always love you."

My unexpected declaration embarrassed Mark, but I decided that was okay. I didn't have much experience in being around young children or finding ways to express what I felt in my heart. My first attempts were bound to be clumsy.

Ever since Ian started to shower me with love, affection, and hope, I felt eager to spill that love out whenever I had the chance. Now that I was finally back in Carlton Heath where the few people in this world that I truly loved resided, I wanted to show them that love, even if the moments turned awkward.

I held onto that thought as I helped finish up the cookies. It was easy to feel and express love for Ellie, Katharine, and Julia. Especially Julia. She kept giving me hugs and saying things like, "I can't wait until you live here all the time, Auntie Miranda."

Once the cookies were done, I had to peel myself away from a clapping game Julia had started. Ellie had sent Mark to Katharine's car for my luggage. She had him transfer it to her car since I'd be staying with them that night. But I intercepted Mark and pulled from my suitcase the items I would need to dress up for the performance later that evening.

As soon as everyone left—Katharine to the hospital and Ellie and the kids home to dress for the play—I took a quick shower and an even quicker ten-minute nap. Then I changed into the special dress I had brought for the performance that evening.

Last year when I attended the play, Ellie was dressed as a Sugar Plum Fairy. I still had sparkles from her ensemble on my peacoat. Katharine had been adorned as a regal lady of the theater. All my clothes were waiting for me in a London hotel room last year, so I attended in my crumpled travel clothes.

This year I couldn't wait to join the merriment by dressing up in my new cheery-cherry-swishy-merry red Christmas dress. I returned to the kitchen for some soup Katharine had left for me on the stove. A note on the kitchen counter reminded me that the Whitcombe family driver would come for me at 6:40.

I had just finished the soup when I heard the door bells jingle.

"I'll be right there!" I called out, placing my soup bowl in the sink.

Heavy-booted footsteps crossed the uneven wooden floor coming toward the kitchen. Apparently the Whitcombe's driver hadn't heard me so I called out again, "You didn't have to come get me!"

The kitchen curtain parted and a magnificent, deep voice rumbled, "Oh yes I did." In front of me in all his white-haired, velvet-robed glory stood Father Christmas.

Chapter Ten

For the briefest of moments, it seemed I was looking at *the* Father Christmas. Tilting my head and studying the eyes, I said, "Ian?"

"Ian to you. Father Christmas to all the wee girls and boys." With a pause he opened his palms and asked, "What do you think? Other than that I must be daft to have agreed to do this."

"No, not at all. You look fantastic! Very convincing. The beard is so believable. Does it itch?"

"I think you would be the one to best answer that question." Ian drew me close and kissed me good. "Well? What's your answer, woman?"

"My answer?"

"Does the beard itch?"

"Oh." I quickly put away the flitting thought that he was asking for an "answer" because he had included a proposal somewhere in the kiss, but I had been too swept up to hear it.

"Actually," I said, regaining my coy composure, "I'm not sure. You better try the kiss test one more time."

Ian willingly obliged.

We drew apart, and I said, "I'm still not quite sure..."

Another kiss came to me as visions of spending the rest of my life with this man danced in my head.

Margaret's driver found Ian and me in the middle of test kiss number four. Neither of us had heard him enter the Tea Cosy. We untangled from our hug and hid our smiles.

Ian addressed the driver somberly. "I'll be taking Miranda to the theatre. Sorry you didn't get the update."

The chauffer tipped his black cap and left us to our kitchen canoodling. Our kiss was short and sweet, followed by a tiny kiss on the end of my nose.

Reaching for my hands and standing back to look at me at arm's length, all Ian said was, "Miranda, you..."

"You like my new dress?"

"The dress is lovely, but it's the beautiful woman wearing the dress I'm in love with."

We paused a moment, standing hand in hand, making mushy eyes at each other, and then I laughed.

"What?" Ian seemed to have forgotten he was dressed as Father Christmas.

"Your outfit is equally ravishing," I said. "But it's the amazing, handsome man wearing the Father Christmas costume I'm in love with."

"So it's not a one-sided crush I'm having on you then, is it?" Ian sneaked in another kiss on the cheek.

I giggled. "Now that one tickled. And the answer to your question is the crush is terminal and highly mutual."

"We'd better get out of here then. Where's your coat?"

I strolled with Father Christmas to his Austin-Healy parked

in front of the Tea Cosy. We zigged down the narrow lane and parked in back of Grey Hall.

Last Christmas I had walked to Grey Hall from the train station and approached the Victorian-style building on a wide walkway lit by eight metal shepherd's hooks. A lantern hung from each hook, twinkling in the dark night. Before me, decked out in long garlands of evergreen boughs, was the theater my father had built during the late 1980s in a style reminiscent of Dickens.

As memorable as that arrival had been, this year with Ian, slipping in through the back entrance was memorable for other reasons. This time the only "décor" I noticed were the faces of the young performers as they watched Father Christmas swoosh past them and head for center stage behind the thick, blue curtain.

Ian pulled out a stack of index cards and stood on his mark, concentrating on getting the lines down. In less than twenty minutes those curtains would part and he would be "it" — the opening performer. All eyes would be on Ian, my Ian, and he would convince them he was Father Christmas.

I knew he could do it.

I blew him a kiss and wiggled my way through the maze of props backstage. If I wanted to, I could find the side door that would take me out to the front of the auditorium. But it seemed more fitting to go out the way we had come in, walk around to the front of Grey Hall, and promenade up the wide path lit with the hanging lanterns on the shepherd's hooks. In a way, I was giving tribute to my father for the theater he had built, as well as giving tribute to my mother who always let me sneak around backstage with her before a performance.

Engaging Father Christmas

What a difference I felt over the way I had approached this theater last Christmas. I had made peace with the thought that my mother loved the theater as much as she loved me. I had come to appreciate the generosity of Sir James to this community, and in a clandestine way, I felt proud to be his daughter.

Entering the bustling lobby, I inched over to the coat check counter. Around me dozens of proud parents chatted with friends, checked their coats, shook hands, and made merry. Ellie was one of the coat checkers this year, which was a little silly due to her petite size. When I stepped up to the window, she was holding three coats and nearly drowned in all the woolen thickness.

"I'll wait until after you hang those up," I said.

"Miranda, look at you! What a beautiful dress. You look absolutely gorgeous! Ian is going to be gobsmacked for certain."

"Gobsmacked?" I repeated with a laugh. "Let me see your outfit."

She handed the stack of coats to her coworker, a tall man in a black top hat and tails, and opened her arms to reveal her surprise ensemble.

"I'm a snowflake," she said. "Can you tell? Someone thought I was trying to be the White Witch of Narnia. I think I may have gotten it all wrong this year."

"Oh, no. You definitely look like a snowflake. I would have guessed snowflake right away."

Her short gown was white with shimmering, pearl-shaded sequins. The sleeves and hem were cut in fanciful, straight-lined snips and clips the way a child cuts a folded-up piece of paper before opening it to reveal a snowflake. She wore white tights, white boots, a sprinkling of iridescent sparkles across her fair skin, and a wreath of white stars around her head.

"Do you think so, really?"

"Definitely. You make a darling snowflake."

"Thank you, Miranda. Have you seen Edward yet? He and Margaret might already be seated. Head toward the front on the left side, and you'll see them. I'll be there shortly."

The usher, dressed in a Nutcracker uniform, handed me a program, and I entered the darkened theater. Fresh boughs of evergreen shaped into huge Christmas wreaths hung from each of the Victorian-style lighting sconces. The ceiling glowed in the amber light, reflecting the inlaid plaster frescos with their repeating oval patterns of soft white-on-white. The dark blue velvet stage curtains were trimmed across the top with golden tassels from which bright red Christmas balls had been hung like holly berries.

Tender memories of my visit last year returned. I think the scent of the pine boughs started the feeling of having come full circle.

When I had reluctantly entered this place a year ago, I still was harboring a deep anger against my mother. Her offense was that the theater was her other love. Acting was her life. And a fall from a faulty balcony on a Venetian set took her life—not only from her but also from me.

After my mother's death, I was raised by Doralee, a bald woman with seven cats named after Egyptian pharaohs. Doralee was one of my mother's theater friends who lived in Santa Cruz where she bravely fought cancer and lost. The incongruous part of it all to me was that she lost with victorious words of heaven on her lips. Doralee was the first Christian I had met and possibly the most peculiar.

My adolescent years in her home fostered an independence that aided me as I faked my age after her death to obtain a job in San Francisco. My strength and independence of the past decade were born out of my silent rebellion against the theater. In some crazy belief birthed in my preteen years and fostered by the vacuum left in my mother's departure from this earth, I thought I could "get back" at the theater if I ignored the place that had been my mother's home and heart.

So I never went to the theater. Nor did I think of it or give it any regard in conversations. This was a challenge while I lived in San Francisco, a place where going to the theater was as much a part of life as going to a restaurant. But I was up to the challenge and remained a devoted boycotter.

Until last Christmas.

I had entered Grey Hall to gain information about my father. But that decision turned out to be the gift I "gave" my mother last Christmas. I said an important good-bye to her that night as I watched vigorous Andrew stride across the stage. I took a first step toward peace inside this theater, which I later discovered had been funded by my father.

Now, a year later, the love of my life was waiting center stage in this same theater, and I entered unencumbered. A nice, round, full circle of peace with the theater encased me in the same way the evergreen wreaths encircled the Victorian-style sconces along the side walls.

I drew in a breath for courage as I walked to the front and stood at the end of the row where Edward and his mother were seated. Seeing them reminded me that I may have made my peace with the theater, but with the two of them, I was walking into a broken circle that I had little hope of repairing. Yet here I was, available. Hopeful. And feeling a little sick to my stomach.

I should have waited for Ellie.

Edward stood in his tall, stiff, professor-like stance and looked at me through the lower portion of his rectangular glasses. Offering his hand, he said, "Good evening, Miranda."

"Good evening, Edward. Good evening, Margaret." I offered my hand to her and let it dangle in the space between us just in case she chose to reach for it. She didn't. Margaret had lightly touched my fingers with a gloved hand when we first met, before she knew who I was. Since then I had been with her half a dozen times, but she had never touched me again. Not once.

Instead of a handshake, Margaret offered me a regal nod. She seemed to be taking in my red dress from top to hem as I stood in the aisle, waiting to be allowed entrance to the Whitcombe row.

I glanced around the quickly filling auditorium in case I would need to find a seat in another row.

Edward, in his usual gentlemanly form, said, "Would you care to sit with us, Miranda?"

"Yes. Thank you."

I slid past Edward and Margaret and was about to leave the seat beside her empty for Ellie when I decided I would attempt to move closer to Margaret both figuratively and literally. I reminded myself of how she had complimented me on my discretion at the Tea Cosy. I also remembered how the other women at the Tea Cosy whispered about her aloofness. From much experience, I understood the art of trying to remain invisible; I recognized the symptoms in Margaret's demeanor.

I hadn't arrived at a sense of earnest sympathy or genuine compassion for her. But I did understand. And maybe that was enough of a first step, even if Margaret never responded to me in kind.

Which she didn't.

Margaret shifted in her seat and exhaled a disagreeable sound that in the past might have been enough to make me get up and move. This night I was determined in this place of full circles to do everything I could to inch this disconnected ring closer to peace and settled completeness.

When Ellie swished down the aisle a few moments later, she motioned for me to move over one seat. I made the change. As Ellie settled into her seat like a bird in a nest, I leaned back, feeling as if I had at least inched closer to Margaret.

The lights inside the theater flickered on and off, indicating the performance was about to begin. The audience hushed. The lights dimmed. The blue velvet curtains parted.

There stood Ian—my Ian—strong and bold and stunning in his flowing white hair, beard, and fur-lined Father Christmas robe. A wreath of holly now circled his head.

In his left hand he held a staff. He raised his right hand to the audience, allowing the wide velvet sleeve to slide down his brawny forearm. Ian's commanding presence was magnificent.

Andrew would have loved seeing this. I wish he and Katharine were here.

"He's so like Sir James!" Ellie whispered to me.

A tender sweetness came over my heart as I realized that my father wore that same robe and stood on this same stage only a few years ago. I had missed seeing him in this role just as Andrew and Katharine were missing Ian now.

Time and distance seemed to fade. I smiled at Ian the way I used to sit in the front row and smile at my mother.

With a quick glance at Margaret, I wondered if she had a special smile she pulled out for my father every time it was opening night for him. Or did she harbor her own unremitting grudge against the theater?

Oh, Margaret, if only you knew how similar we are. If only you would give me a chance.

Chapter Eleven

an's booming voice rode over the audience like a tidal wave as he delivered the opening line. "Marley was dead. As dead as a doornail."

Ellie reached over and gave my hand a happy squeeze. I squeezed hers back. The play was afoot, and all my attention was center stage. Ian completed his short monologue, stepped to the side, and gave a sweeping gesture to mark the commencement of the first scene. The cast of characters filed on stage beginning with Mark in his Scrooge business suit costume. He launched his first line by yelling at two of the bookkeepers, telling them to work faster.

"You are sorely mistaken if you think I will be giving you the day off for Christmas!" Poor Mark, his preadolescent voice cracked on "sorely mistaken" and "Christmas."

The audience muffled a collective chuckle. I turned to Ellie and saw that she was making a motherly wince. "Keep going, Markie," she whispered.

Mark went right on, undaunted by the wobbly opening. Within minutes he had the audience in the palm of his hand and showed no signs of stage fright. I felt so proud of him. His sense of timing and deadpan expressions proved quickly that he wasn't just the stand-in understudy. He was a natural. He was unmistakably the grandson of Sir James Whitcombe.

By the time the intermission lights came on, it was clear I wasn't the only one bursting with excitement and pride over Mark's performance.

"Your son is brilliant," the woman behind us said, patting Ellie on the shoulder.

"He's doing quite well, isn't he?" Ellie was all smiles. "A bit of vocal range lurch there at the beginning, but he pulled it off, wouldn't you say?"

Edward adjusted his glasses and nodded. I wondered how he really felt about his son's success.

A woman behind Margaret said, "It takes only one such performance to set a course for a lifetime. I dare say your grandson has revived the talent of our own Sir James this evening. Why has the young man not performed before?"

"It was his choice," Edward said firmly.

I had a feeling it might have been a choice strongly influenced by Edward. His affection for the theater and all that came with the life of an actor was as low as mine had been last year.

"Shall we go to the lobby for a bit of a sweet?" Ellie rose from her seat.

Edward and I both went to the lobby with Ellie while Margaret stayed behind. We were soon caught up in the crush of people gathered around the refreshment table. It was fun hearing all the comments about young Mark and his performance.

The good people of Carlton Heath had all come to the same conclusion. Mark was destined to follow in his grandfather's footsteps across the golden stage. Each of them seemed to enjoy announcing that acting was "in his blood," as if they were the first one to arrive at that conclusion.

One woman even had the boldness to say, "The talent obviously didn't fall to you, Edward—no offense meant."

"None taken," he said.

"The talent skipped a generation and has fallen on Mark, wouldn't you say?"

With the audience high on the speculations of young Mark's future on the stage, we returned to our seats and settled in for act two.

The curtains parted and six extras, including Julia, entered dressed as waifs, all wearing nightgowns and sleeping caps that looked like puffed-up muffin tops.

Instead of staying with the pack while Scrooge and the Spirit of Christmas Present visited the workhouse, Julia stepped to the side of the stage and gave a little wave to her mum and dad. Ellie waved back.

Pleased with the ruffle of giggles her antics produced, Miss Julia favored us with a six- year-old, ballerina-style spin around. Her costume filled with air and puffed out. She spun a second time, and Ellie whispered, "Oh dear, she knows better than to be showing off like that."

Pointing her finger at Julia and inching it in the air like a little worm, Ellie silently directed the free-spirited waif back to where she belonged on stage.

Clever Mark ad-libbed the obvious interruption with a quick quip. He glared at his sister with his hand on his hip and said, "Oh, Spirit of Christmas Present, it seems you're not the only spirit sent to torment me this night."

The crowd laughed. Mark broke character just long enough to turn to his mum and dad and offer a shrug. He squared his shoulders and went on with his next line without missing a beat.

Julia, not having caught the implication, looked at the audience with a grand smile, as if she were the source of all the merriment. As soon as she was offstage, she found her way through the back of the hall and came to our aisle. Margaret held out her arms for Julia to sit on her lap.

Julia demurely slid past her grandmother. I was surprised since Julia and her grandmother shared a close and sweet relationship. But Julia was definitely "mummy's girl," so when she edged her way past her grandmother, I thought she was going to cuddle up with Ellie.

Instead, Julia headed straight for me. She invited herself up into my lap and settled in as if this were the only place in the world she wanted to be.

Julia whispered to her mother and me, asking if we saw her spinning on stage.

"Yes, darling," Elli whispered to her overeager thespian. "Now hush. We mustn't talk until the play is over."

I glanced at Margaret. If she was miffed that Julia had come to me instead of her, she didn't show it in her expression. The rest of the play I tried not to think of Margaret but instead concentrated on enjoying the delight of having my cuddly niece on my lap and my clever nephew on the stage.

Before the fall of the curtain, Ian returned to his mark, center stage. With grand, Father Christmas hand motions, he had a final word for the merry audience.

"I charge you, gentlefolk, far and wide,
Heed this tale as told you this night.
Whenever you happen upon those in need,
Look to your heart and do a good deed.
Gather close this Christmastide,
All your loved ones by your side.
Mother, father, daughter, son,
May God bless us, everyone!"

The crowd erupted in applause. A standing ovation followed as the entire cast assembled onstage. Julia apparently had forgotten she would be given this additional chance to be in the spotlight.

She couldn't scamper off my lap quickly enough and charged up the narrow side steps in her flowing waif nightclothes. She joined her brother in the lineup. Mark did an admirable job of sharing his big moment with his little sister.

The houselights went up, and Ian fixed his gentle gaze on me. I blew him a kiss. He stayed in character and simply gave me a nod of his snowy head. I couldn't wait to see the magic that I knew would happen in the lobby when the little children would have a chance to sit on his lap and have their photos taken.

As we filed out of the row, I sidled up to Edward. "Was it

here that you had the photo taken on your father's lap when he was dressed as Father Christmas?"

"I don't recall where the infamous Christmas photo was taken. It was quite some time ago. Do you remember, Mother?"

Margaret needed for Edward to repeat the question to her. She thought a moment and then shook her head. "No, the doors to my memory on such details seem to have lost a few of their keys."

I smiled at Margaret in response to her comment and gave her a warm and open gaze. I wanted her to see that my hope for the door that had been unlocked between us earlier at the Tea Cosy would remain unlocked.

She didn't smile back. She looked the other way, and when we arrived in the lobby, Edward arranged for the driver to take her home.

The rest of the lobby was humming with activity. Parents on all sides were congratulating each other for their children's performances. Buoyant cast members were taking advantage of the table spread.

I watched Mark as he stood tall and straight, receiving a steady stream of handshakes and accolades.

Making my way to the other side of the lobby, I joined the parents and children who had stepped into a line, instinctively forming a queue to have a chat or a photo with Father Christmas. Ian was seated on a high-backed chair that was trimmed with evergreen and red ribbons.

I stood to the side, trying to suppress my grin as I watched Ian with the children. He poured on the charm, holding babies, letting them pull on his beard, or leaning over to listen to toddlers as they whispered in his ear.

He *was* Father Christmas.

For fun, I got in line too. Ian looked up and noticed where I was standing. He winked at me, and I understood I didn't have to wait in line. Ian already knew what I wanted for Christmas. As a matter of fact, I had a pretty good feeling my wish was at the top of his list.

Chapter Twelve

e're thinking of going to hospital," Ellie said, coming up beside me after most of the hubbub in the lobby had calmed down. "Edward hasn't paid a visit to Andrew yet. We thought we might all pop over instead of going directly home. Do you and Ian have plans for a trip to hospital as well?"

"I'm not sure what we're going to do. Should I call you after Ian is finished here?"

"No need. We're not ready to leave just yet. The children are enjoying their moment of glory. A bit too much, Edward thinks, but how often will such an event occur?"

Ellie flitted off to finish her obligations in the coat room while I strolled over to the refreshment table to see if I could do anything to help clean up.

A woman dressed in a hilarious penguin costume, complete with a long beak, said, "Oh, no, we have it all covered, dear, but thanks ever so for offering. You're the friend of the Whitcombes, aren't you?"

"Yes. I'm Miranda."

"We think your beau did a lovely job as Father Christmas."

"I'll tell him you said so. Your costume is . . ." I hadn't selected my descriptive word ahead of time and nearly couldn't find the right one. " . . . charming."

"I'm the Christmas penguin, you see."

I didn't know any stories about Christmas penguins, so I apologized for my lack of familiarity with British Christmas tales and asked her to explain.

"Oh, there's no explanation, really. This was the only costume I had!"

I laughed with her, and we joked about how she could start a new tradition.

Flora from the Tea Cosy stepped close and entered into the conversation as if she had been with us from the beginning and, having stepped away for a moment, she now had returned. She had quite a talent for slicing into conversations that way.

"My, that was an interesting young man at the Cosy this afternoon, wasn't he?" Flora looked at me through her large, round glasses.

I gave her a noncommittal nod.

"The bag he carried was altogether ominous, though, wouldn't you agree?"

I nodded again.

"I understand he carried it with him to the train station, got on the 3:22 for London, and who knows what he's up to now. Good riddance, I say."

Clearly Flora's sources were on the job that afternoon, all the way to the train station, to give her a full report.

"We don't need his sort around here, do we? No one quite

seems to know why he came here. You wouldn't happen to know, would you?"

My wonderful knight in shining velvet robes came to my rescue at just the right moment. He greeted the women, received their compliments, and politely asked if he might steal me from their company.

The Christmas penguin was agreeable, but Flora made it clear she had hoped for a longer visit.

As Ian and I stepped away from the ladies, I said, "You came at just the right time."

"Did I now? You weren't getting uncomfortable talking about Josh, were you?"

I looked up at him. "You heard."

"Of course I heard." With a twinkle in his eye, he added, "Christmas wishes weren't the only secrets whispered in my ear once I put on these robes."

"What did you hear?"

"Only that the menacing, ski-cap stalker followed you here, engaged you in a brief conversation, had some tea and scones — with jam and cream, by the way — and left on the next train to London."

I laughed at his rundown. "You got it all straight then. Except for one addition."

"What's that?"

"Josh wanted to know if I was taken."

Ian raised one of his stage-makeup, white, bushy eyebrows. "And what did you tell him?"

"I told him I was practically engaged to Father Christmas, and if he didn't get out of town, you would run him over with your reindeer."

"Did you, now?"

Nudging Ian to the side of the lobby, as far away from any possible eavesdroppers as possible, I said, "I told Josh something else, and I need you to know about it."

Ian's bushy eyebrows dipped, expressing his concentration in what I was about to say but exaggerating the expression in such a way that made the moment seem more dramatic than I thought it should be.

In a whisper, I said, "I told Josh who my father was."

Now Ian's eyebrows lifted in an equally exaggerated fashion, almost causing me to laugh. I knew what I was telling him wasn't a laughing matter.

"I felt I could tell him since he was the one who first urged me to come to Carlton Heath after seeing the photo of my dad dressed as Father Christmas. I trust Josh to keep the confidence."

"Are you sure you can trust him?"

"Yes. He's a psychologist. He keeps confidences for a living. I just wanted you to know. And as far as his visit to the Tea Cosy, I'm convinced it was more about satisfying his curiosity concerning Carlton Heath and the chance to add a few more hours of adventure to his ski trip than it was about me. That's how he is."

"You're sure, then, that I don't need to hunt him down and make it clear he doesn't have a chance to reconcile with you?"

"You don't need to hunt him down. We don't have any reconciling to do. All is settled."

"You're sure?"

I nodded. "I'm sure."

I never had a brave defender like Ian in my life before. I kind of liked his expressions of eagerness to protect me. His valor seemed a little more believable, though, when he wasn't looking at me with two snow-white caterpillars appearing as if they were doing push-ups on his eyebrows.

Mark dashed up to us at that moment, his face flushed with the rush of the sudden glory. "Are we leaving soon?"

"We're ready if you are," Ian said.

"Mark, you did such a fantastic job. I'm so proud of you."

"Thank you, Aunt Miranda." He seemed to emphasize the "Aunt" just enough for me to catch his meaning.

I smiled, and he smiled back. The lump in my throat didn't go down easily.

"Mark and I will bring the car round to the front," Ian said.

"Okay. I'll meet you out there in a few minutes." I returned to pick up my coat from among the few left hanging in the coatroom and then stepped out into the chilly night air.

A jolly sight greeted me. Father Christmas was behind the wheel of his convertible sports car with the top down. Mark was perched on the top like a celebrity in a parade, ready to wave to loyal fans as he passed by at two miles per hour. Both men were once again receiving the accolades due after such memorable debuts.

I slipped in on the passenger's side only after excusing my way through the final circle of adoring fans. This gathering of merry-eyed girls in the preteen bracket gazed at Mark with unalterable admiration. His life in this small village would never be the same.

"Will you sign my program?" one of the girls asked.

I pulled a pen from my purse and watched Mark enjoy his moment in the moonlight.

Once the giggling flock scattered, Ian started the engine. As soon as it began to rumble, Ian waved his hand so that the wide sleeve of his brocaded robe flapped like a great bird.

"Good night, Father Christmas!" one of the preteens called out, igniting another round of giggles from her chums.

"Happy Christmas to you all," he called, as we drove out of sight.

The cool, rushing breeze chilled me instantly even though Ian had the car's heater going. Mark was full of glee over his newly acquired fame and found happiness in scrunching into the narrow storage space behind the seats, lifting both hands in the air, and shouting, "Whoo-hoo!" for the first two blocks.

Ian and I exchanged smiles. Watching Mark was too fun to tell him to stop. Every child should feel that happy, that free.

Ian leaned over. "I'll take a dozen. Just like him."

With a cunning grin I replied, "I think you'll need a bigger car."

Ian laughed his deep-hearted laugh, and our merry mobile headed over a ridge. We turned on the cutoff road that led toward the old church.

From behind a stately rise of the unaltered medieval forest, we saw it, all at the same moment. The golden moon. That eternal orb, broken in half, teetering in the velvet night like a crown cast at the foot of a throne.

Ian stopped the car. The engine purred. The three of us stared without speaking.

Mark sat up straight in his seat of honor and quietly sang in Latin. I have never heard anything so piercingly beautiful.

His boys' choir voice wasn't cooperative on the high notes,

but it didn't matter. Mark wasn't performing now. It was just us—Ian, me, Father God, and all the hosts of heaven bending down to listen to a song that rose from a true heart.

Ian took my hand, and a line from a Christmas carol rode over the top of Mark's canticle, blending perfectly. *Let heaven and nature sing....*

At that moment, I felt as if I were experiencing a snapshot of heaven. The glorious beauty and sense of perfection and wonder felt like a glimpse of that which is true and lasting. It was as if I were viewing a wallet-sized photo of eternity.

For so many years I had gazed at the snapshot of my father. The photo, in all its curious wonder, was still only a flat, frozen image of a real person I had never met. The photo carried with it a clue about a place called "Carlton Heath."

Now here I was, experiencing the immenseness of Carlton Heath in all of its beauty. It was far beyond the sketchy speculations that had risen in my imagination from the one simple photo.

As Mark's voice rose into the night air, I wondered, was everything around us more or less a fixed snapshot that alluded to a greater beauty? A deeper mystery? A hint of what was to come? How many unknown layers were there to life—to the eternal life that was hidden in Christ? What glorious surprises awaited us in the real land of which this earth was only a snapshot?

Let heaven and nature sing....

Mark's song ended on a note that he sustained much longer than I would have thought possible. Then all was silent except for the low rumble of the car's engine.

Without any of us trying to define what had just taken

place, Ian edged the car back on the road and continued our short journey to the hospital.

I watched the moon as we drove down the lane and thought of how the upturned golden curve of light resembled a smile. I liked the imagery that Father God was pleased with our spontaneous worship and was smiling down on us.

Keep smiling, Father God. Keep smiling on us, I pray.

Mark scooted down into the narrow space behind the bucket seats and bundled up in a plaid wool blanket Ian earlier had pulled from the trunk. My guess was that Ian made the blanket available just in case Mark came down from his high and needed more than his fame to warm him.

The blanket was the MacGregor tartan, of course. I remembered the blanket fondly from a picnic Ian and I had last summer. We took off with plans to spend the day on the coast of southern England. I wanted to picnic beneath the fabulous White Cliffs of Dover. However, we only made it as far as Windsor before the car began to sputter. Ian found a repair service, and we spent the day strolling around the castle grounds, waiting for the fuel line to be replaced.

Ellie had packed us a picnic lunch, which we carried along with the MacGregor plaid blanket to a grassy knoll on the public grounds of Windsor Castle. There, within view of the British guards with their tall fur hats strapped under their chins, I learned about the MacGregor crest and the clan motto, "Royal is my race."

As Ian turned the steering wheel and headed for the hospital on this cold winter night, it did indeed seem as if he was part of a "royal race." His white hair and beard shone in the moonlight. All the gold and silver trimming on his robe stood out with regal shimmers. His jaw was set. His face directed straight ahead. The Scottish warrior was on his way to see his father.

All was calm. All was bright.

Oh, how I wanted to believe this was how life was going to be. Once I had a few significant pieces of the plans for my future lined up, I could nestle into this place of beauty and hope. Carlton Heath was not yet fully my home, but I wanted it to be — soon.

Chapter Thirteen

he hospital staff at the front desk had big smiles and hellos for us when we entered and they saw Ian in full costume.

"What did you bring us, Father Christmas?" the admitting nurse asked.

"Good cheer and merry greetings," he said in a robust voice. Some of the faithful employees seemed to be looking behind Ian for his sack of gifts. A childlike shadow of disappointment crossed their faces when they didn't see a bag slung over his shoulder filled with goodies.

"We do have biscuits left over from the play tonight," Mark said. "My mum is bringing them."

A few minutes after Mark announced the biscuits, Ellie, Edward, and Julia entered the hospital carrying the promised goodies.

The lobby suddenly became cheerier. Night staff appeared from behind swinging doors and file cabinets.

"We're going to visit my father," Ian said to the head nurse. "You won't mind if we're above the limit for visitors, will you?"

Ellie held out the bag of cookies as potential bribe material.

"We'll look the other way this time." She reached for one of the shortbread stars. "Katharine is already in there."

Ian led the way down the hall of the quiet hospital. Mark looked up at the sign that read Children's Ward over the doorway of the first wing we passed. As we kept walking, Mark asked Ian, "Are children staying in there, in the children's ward, tonight?"

"I would imagine so."

"Will they be going home for Christmas?"

"Perhaps. If they're too ill, though, they will be staying here."

Julia, who had been holding my hand as we made our way down the hall, asked, "If the children don't go home for Christmas, how will they get any presents?"

"I'm sure they receive their presents here," Ellie said in her optimistic voice.

Mark stopped walking. "How many children are in the children's ward?"

"Hard to say," Ian said.

"We need to find out how many children there are, and we need to bring them some presents," Mark said decisively.

"That's very considerate of you, Mark," Ellie said. "It's a lovely idea. First, we must pay a visit to Uncle Andrew, though. Shall we do that? We can check on the children's ward on our way out."

Mark picked up his feet, still deep in thought. All six of us entered Andrew's room quietly. As soon as weary Katharine saw us, she motioned for us to enter and come closer.

"How's the patient?" Ian asked.

Andrew's distinct voice rose from the bed. "The patient is growing impatient. That's how the patient is."

We gathered around, all saying our hellos at once. The rhythmic drips and beeps of the machines seemed as hypnotizing as a swinging pocket watch. Andrew's deep-chested breathing carried the steady ruffles of air flowing in and out at a comforting pace.

"You're looking more yourself than you did earlier," Ellie said.

"Am I, now?" Andrew smiled weakly.

He looked up at Ian in the convincing costume and added, "What's this? A visit from the man himself?"

"It's really Uncle Ian," Julia said with a twinkling grin.

"Is that so? Well, I was convinced he was Father Christmas himself."

Julia giggled.

"The role is only temporary," Ian said. "You do know that you're expected to pick up where you left off next Christmas, don't you? I was only a fill-in."

"Aye, you've been talking to Katharine, haven't you? She refuses to accept my resignation."

"Good for her," I said.

"The play went off wonderfully well," Ellie said. "But you were missed."

"Mark was the star of the show," I said. "And Julia was superb."

Both children beamed in the light of the praise as Andrew added, "Good job, you two."

His eyelids drooped. Apparently he had used up all his personal visiting hours and was ready to sleep some more and heal.

"You are getting better, aren't you?" Julia patted Andrew's shoulder.

"Yes, Uncle Andrew is getting better," Ellie answered. "We should let him rest. He's had a very long day."

We said our good-byes to a sleepy-eyed Andrew and made our way out of the room.

"Father," Mark reached for Edward's arm as soon as we were out the door. "May we go for a visit in the children's ward now?"

Edward and Ellie looked surprised that Mark hadn't forgotten his request on the way in and dropped the subject.

"We really should be on our way home," Ellie said. "It's been a long day. And tomorrow is Christmas Eve, after all."

"Yes, but, Mummy, what about the children here at hospital? Tomorrow is Christmas Eve for them as well. Not all of them will be going home for Christmas, though, will they?"

"Possibly they will," Ellie said hopefully.

"I think we should visit them the way we visited Uncle Andrew. It won't take long."

The rest of us looked at each other, trying to gauge our collective thoughts on the possibility. I hadn't realized Mark was a young man of such compassion.

"Look," Mark continued as firmly as a diplomat, "Uncle Ian is already dressed like Father Christmas. Why could he not take some gifts to the children tonight?"

"Yes, Mummy!" Julia tugged on Ellie's hand. "Can we do it, please?"

Edward was facing Katharine. "I would imagine Father Christmas already has made his rounds for this year in the children's ward."

Katharine shook her head. No alternate Father Christmas had come. Since my father had played that role in years past, it seemed no replacement had picked up the part.

"Well," Ellie said brightly, "how about if next Christmas we make a visit to the children's ward as a family project? We'll have time to pick lots of presents. And we'll bake lots and lots of biscuits. Won't that be lovely?"

"We can't wait for next Christmas," Mark said firmly. "Not all the children in there will get better, will they? This might be their last Christmas."

Mark's evaluation seemed to hit all of us in the same soft spot in our hearts.

Edward remained the voice of reason. "We aren't prepared this year, though, Mark. We don't have gifts for the children. If we plan for next year, we can arrange to have lots of gifts. That would be better, wouldn't it?"

Julia gave a little wiggle-hop. "Mummy, you can give the children my presents. I don't need any new toys." Her sincere expression was enough to melt any heart.

The first heart it apparently melted was her daddy's. "I suppose..."

"The children can have all of my gifts as well," Mark added.

Edward appeared too choked up at the moment to respond.

Clearing his throat, he said, "Ian, would you mind keeping the costume on a bit longer?"

"Not at all," Ian said robustly.

"Right, then. It looks as if we'll be back shortly with some gifts to distribute."

Chapter Fourteen

By the time the Whitcombe clan returned to the hospital with all the gifts and a round of rosy cheeks, it was after ten. The excitement had kept the children going. Ellie had managed to tuck two dozen gifts into a large laundry sack. Edward looked more invigorated than I had ever seen him. I was seeing an entirely new view of my half brother and finding he wasn't as stodgy as I had thought.

I knew his father—our father—convincingly carried out the role of Father Christmas right up until he passed away. Locals told tender stories of how they had whispered their Christmas wish into Father Christmas's ear when they were tiny and how, magically, their wishes always came true.

Now it was Ian's turn. He adjusted his beard and the holly wreath on his head. Ellie brushed off the lint from his brocaded velvet robe, and Ian slung the laundry sack over his broad shoulders. Mark and Julia flanked his sides, and the rest of us trailed him as an unconventional group of elves.

"I've brought my camera," Ellie said with a sugarplum twinkle in her eye. "Might be a lovely gift for the parents, don't you think? Snapshots of the look on their children's faces when they see Father Christmas."

"What a great idea, Ellie."

A gathering of night nurses and a doctor stood waiting for us at the door that opened to the children's ward. They ushered us in, and Ian's deep, golden voice called out into the dimly lit hallway, "Happy Christmas, one and all!"

A nurse adjusted the light switch so that the ward glowed with a Christmas morning sort of brightness. Through the doors we could see the children rubbing their eyes and trying to see what was going on. One of them, a little girl in a neck brace, was the first to get a full view of Ian. Her squeal alerted the entire ward as she called out, "It's Father Christmas!"

Ellie snapped pictures. Edward hung back, his eyes looking tenderer than I had ever seen. I wondered if in his childhood he had been like Mark, accompanying Sir James in his Father Christmas robe. Was Christmas a time of tender memories for my half brother?

Ian and Julia strode over to the bedside of the delighted little girl in the neck brace. Ellie kept snapping pictures. Mark assisted Father Christmas by looking for a gift inside the sack.

"That one." Julia pointed to a present wrapped in paper that was dotted with silver stars and tied with a pink ribbon.

The little girl's eyes were wide as she stared at Father Christmas. "I hoped you would come. I was afraid you wouldn't know where I was."

"I've come indeed. And I have a gift for you," he said.

"Open it!" excited Julia said.

The dazzled little sweetheart didn't seem to be able to over-come her amazement enough to tear the wrapping paper from the box. "May I hold it for a while?"

"You may hold it as long as you like." Ian placed his hand on the girl's forehead and said, "God bless you this day, dear child. You are His special gift. May He hold you ever close to His heart."

She closed her eyes and eagerly received the blessing. As we left her room, the darling was still hugging the silvery box with her eyes closed and her lips pressed into an endearing smile.

We went from room to room down the hall and watched Julia and Mark as they assisted Ian in distributing gifts. Ellie snapped dozens of photos. Ian placed his hand on each child and blessed each one. Every child responded differently, but all of them seemed mesmerized and delighted. Even the older children.

In one of the last rooms we entered, a boy who looked to be about ten years old stared at the doorway. The pillow behind him seemed to be swallowing his bald head. His mother sat beside him, holding his hand and telling him what was happening. "He's come into your room now, Bobby. It's Father Christmas! Do you see him? He's come to see you! It's Father Christmas!"

The young boy was too weak to respond with more than a slight rising of his upper lip. Ian went to his side.

"Happy Christmas, young Bobby. My helpers and I have brought you a gift."

"Can you see his white beard, Bobby?" the mother said. "And the wreath of holly on his head. Do you want to feel his robe? Here. Look at the velvet trim stitched in gold. Very regal, isn't it?"

The little boy's hand lifted and rested on Ian's arm. A brightness appeared in his eyes. I wondered if the weakened state of this poor child would be too much for Mark and Julia to handle, but both of them moved closer instead of shrinking back.

Ellie continued snapping pictures. The tenderhearted mother, with her face glowing in the diffused light, leaned over her son and helped him engage with Father Christmas.

"Father Christmas has brought you a gift," Mark said. "Shall I help you open it?"

The boy nodded weakly. His delighted expression was fixed. Mark opened the gift, and I saw him hesitate as if this was the one item he had wished for and now it was going to this frail child.

"It's a junior microscope." Mark held up the box.

The boy's chest quavered, and he released breathy, happy sounds and reached for the box.

His mother looked up at Ian and the rest of us. With a stunned expression she said, "How did you know? You couldn't possibly have known. That's all he's wanted for months. How did you know?"

"We didn't know," Julia said plainly.

All of us tried very hard to keep our wobbling lips from giving away how surprised and touched we were.

I felt as I had when we watched the moon in Ian's car. Leaning closer to the mother, I said, "This is the part of Christmas when we can hear heaven and nature sing."

She nodded. "Bobby, tell Father Christmas what you want to be when you grow up."

With an expansive exhale, Bobby wheezed, "A doctor."

I looked at Ian and saw two glistening tears race down his ruddy cheeks, dampening his beard. All of us, except perhaps Julia, realized it would take a miracle for Bobby to win the battle against whatever it was that had invaded his young body. The chances were slim that he would live long enough to become a doctor.

Katharine drew close to Bobby's mother and placed her calm hand on the woman's shoulders. This was what Katharine did best. She was a comforter. This mother's Christmas gift was having Katharine there with her at this moment to support her.

Ian reached out his hand and placed it on Bobby's forehead. He blessed the young boy and continued with a prayer, asking the Lord to heal his body and to fulfill all His purposes for Bobby's life.

Edward stepped out of the room, and I wasn't far behind him. I felt a reservoir of tears building up, and I wasn't sure I could contain them. Sniffing and swallowing in the corner, I saw Edward speaking with one of the doctors. He was handing over his business card. I heard him say, "Whatever expenses this family doesn't have taken care of, I would like to cover. Anonymously."

"Yes, of course," the doctor said. "I did this often for your father. I know how to proceed."

At that point, all I wanted to do was crumble into a chair and weep.

But Ian and the children were on the move. We had one

more patient to visit. Her name was Molly. When she saw Julia, the two recognized each other.

"What happened to you, Molly?" Julia asked.

"I had my index taken out two days ago. Do you want to see the bandage?" Molly pulled back the covers and revealed a large gauze patch on her side where her appendix apparently had been removed.

"Did it hurt?" Julia asked.

Molly nodded.

"Do you feel better now?"

"A little."

"Good because we brought Father Christmas to see you." Julia pointed at Ian as if Molly hadn't noticed the larger-than-life figure standing behind her. "And we brought you a present, too."

Molly smiled at Ian. "I know who you are," she said in a whisper.

He put his finger to his lips and indicated that she should keep her voice low. "You will keep our secret, won't you?"

Molly nodded.

Mark pulled a gift from the sack for Molly. "Happy Christmas."

"Happy Christmas to you too. Thank you for the present." She tore off the wrapping paper and gave a small "ohh!" of glee when she saw the picture on the outside of the box. "It's the singing teapot! I wanted one of these very badly."

By the expression on Julia's face, it was clear that, just like her brother, she had given away the gift she had hoped for. With a quavering lower lip, she said, "I always wanted one too." She looked to her mother, and Ellie gave her a pacifying expression.

I quelled a happy smile because I had purchased the exact same singing teapot for Julia in San Francisco. It was in my suitcase now and would be under the tree at Ellie and Edward's by tomorrow. Julia would have her singing teapot after all.

Ian stepped over to the bed and placed his hand on Molly to give her the final Christmas blessing in the children's ward. Ellie snapped the picture and then our entourage made its way back to the lobby. A chorus of "Thank you," "Happy Christmas," and "Good-bye, Father Christmas" followed us to the door. The night staff added their expressions of appreciation with smiles and tears.

"Well, we best be on our way," Ellie said. "What a night, for all of us!"

A bit dazed, we all filed into our cars. Ian had put the top up on his, and when I climbed into the passenger's seat, I pulled the plaid blanket over me. "I'm going to close my eyes for just a minute," I announced as I felt the jet lag settle into my bones.

The next thing I remembered was the back of Ian's rough hand tenderly stroking my cheek and his deep voice saying, "Miranda, we're here."

Chapter Fifteen

barely remember Ian ushering me into the Whitcombe manor late that night and carrying my luggage up to the guest room. I do remember Ian's warm kiss good night, his whisper in my ear and how it was filled with promise. He said he would see me in the morning. That in itself was a dream. We were together on the same side of the globe and would be only a hop and a skip away from each other. Not an ocean away.

My dreams that night in the comfy guest bed Ellie had made ready for me must have been the sort of dreams I had rehearsed many times over during the past year. I floated from one happiness to another and sank deeply into the kind of rest that restores and renews.

I found out later that poor little Julia was beside herself by ten thirty the next morning. She had waited so patiently for me to wake up, and I was fast asleep every time she checked.

When I finally awoke, I went to the thick-paned window and

looked out at a gray, dark world that made it seem much earlier in the morning than it was. Grumpy old clouds bundled in their heavy winter coats bumped into each other and crowded the sky, stubbornly refusing to let the sun peek through.

I stretched and felt luxuriously rested but chilled.

Dashing back to bed, I heard a tap on my door.

"Who is it?"

"It's Ju-lee-ah," my favorite niece sang out. She must have heard me rustling about. When I told her she could come in, she peeked around the door with a hopeful grin. I held out my arms and smiled. She jumped up on the bed while I admired her freshly combed hair, pulled back with a red ribbon on the side. Her sweater was also red with a row of little Christmas trees around the cuffs and collar.

"Don't you look cute this morning?"

"This is my Christmas Eve Day sweater. I have a different one for Christmas Day to wear with my new Christmas skirt. What are you wearing for today and for Christmas?"

"I'm not sure yet. Something warm. It's cold, isn't it?"

"Yes. Cold and rainy. We've had our breakfast already, Auntie Miranda. You were the sleepyhead, weren't you? Mummy said we may do whatever we wish because Uncle Ian called, and he's not ready yet so you must stay with us until he's ready."

"Is that so?"

"Would you like to have your breakfast in bed? Because Mummy said if you want to eat in bed, Natasha can bring up a tray, and I can have tea with you."

"Who is Natasha?"

"She's our new helper. She has red shoes, and she wears

them even when it isn't Christmas. Have you seen our beautiful Christmas tree yet? It's the biggest tree we've ever had. Daddy and Markie and I went to the forest, and we were supposed to cut down our Christmas tree last week, but when we got into the forest, I started to cry."

"Why? What happened?"

"I didn't want to cut any of the trees down, so we left without one. And do you know what Mummy did the next day?"

"Let me guess. Your mom went to the forest and cut down a tree all by herself and dragged it home to surprise all of you."

"No, silly! My mummy couldn't do all that."

I wouldn't it put it past Ellie.

"Mummy went to a store where they have pretend trees that look even more real than real trees. She bought the very biggest one they had, and now every year we get to have the same very big tree for Christmas. And I put the star on the top. Do you want to come see it now? It's the most beautiful tree in the whole world."

"The most beautiful tree in the *whole* world?"

"Yes." Julia giggled and gave a resolute nod of her head. "It is the most beautiful tree in the whole world. Do you want to come see it?"

"First, I have something very important to do."

"What?"

"I must give you your morning tickle. Come here." I wrapped my arms around my favorite little chatter bug, and before I commenced with the tickling, I said, "I love you, Julia-Bean. I love you, love you, love you."

"I'm not a bean."

"Yes you are. You're my little Julia-Bean. Whenever one of your little Julia-Bean giggles gets planted in my heart, it grows and grows and grows until it's so big that everywhere I look all I see is happiness!"

She seemed surprised at my silliness and expressions of affection, but she received them by glibly offering her soft cheek to me so that I might plant the expected kiss on her smooth, pink skin. Instead of one kiss, I tickle-kissed her with a dozen kisses all over her head, cheek, and neck, and so the morning tickle fest began.

Julia squealed gleefully and tried to tickle me back under my chin. Her pudgy little fingers moved like a harpist and made me laugh even though it didn't really tickle.

We called a truce, and she gave me a kiss right on the end of my nose to seal our peace pact. I thought of how Ian had kissed the tip of my nose last night in the Tea Cosy's kitchen, and I realized I had received more kisses, hugs, and snuggles in the past year than I had since my mother died.

I thought of how much my mother would have loved all this. This house, this bed, the sight and sounds of me tickling my niece on Christmas Eve morn. But these riches of Sir James's had not come to her. All she received from her brief love affair with him was me. And now I had managed to slide in and enjoy so much of the goodness of this family.

But for how long?

With our tickle fest over, Julia asked, "What about the tree? When will you come see the tree?"

"How about if get cleaned up first? You can go tell your mom and Natasha that Princess Miranda and Princess Julia would indeed like to take their tea in bed this morning, and Princess Miranda would also like some toast with marmalade."

"Oh yes, I want toast too. With marmalade." Julia slid off the bed. "I'll go tell them. Do you want an egg? We have new Christmas eggcups."

"Well yes, if you have new eggcups, of course I want an egg for breakfast."

"And baked beans and bacon? That's what I had for breakfast."

"Why not?" I said.

Julia was on her way to order what I had come to learn was a typical English breakfast. The first time I saw the baked beans and grilled tomato slices on the breakfast plate next to my over easy eggs and wide strips of lean bacon, I thought it was a joke. Who eats baked beans for breakfast? Well, now I do. Every time I come to Carlton Heath.

Half an hour later, even though Julia and I were both dressed and ready for the day, we slipped back under the puffy comforter in our stockinged feet and stacked up the pillows behind us so we would be nice and comfy. We waited like two little princesses with our hands folded on top of the comforter as timid Natasha entered the room with a heavy tray laden with our breakfast delights.

Once she saw that Julia and I were in the silliest of moods, she smiled and helped me balance the tray on my lap before quietly exiting and leaving Julia and me to our feast. We had a stack of well-toasted bread that required marmalading. We had a steaming teapot wrapped in a quilted tea cozy and ready to be tipped over and poured into our waiting china cups.

Marvelously and perhaps miraculously, we managed all the finer details of our feast without a single spill or drip of orange marmalade on the bed.

Our voices were low as we talked, tucked away in the warm bed in that spacious bedroom in the Whitcombe manor. Mostly Julia talked, and I listened. She had much to tell me about the Christmas gifts she had helped wrap, the vase she and Daddy bought for Ellie, and how she knew where Mummy had hidden the Christmas crackers this year.

Memories of my sparse Christmas mornings with my mother came to mind. She and I also cuddled up in bed and talked softly. I suppose I thought I was a princess then too. My mother and I certainly had no maid to bring us toast on a silver tray. We mostly lived in budget motels during my formative years. The blankets were thin, and the sheets were cold and rough and smelled of bleach.

I remembered how I would find ways to wrap up the tiny soaps and shampoos allotted to us in the nicer budget motels. Those were my gifts to my mother on Christmas morning as we curled up together in bed. She always responded with such surprise and pleasure when she opened the soaps and shampoo as if I had given her something of great worth that she actually wanted or needed.

My mother always had a box of chocolates for us at Christmas. I don't know if the chocolates were given to her or if she bought them, but that's what we ate for breakfast. As many decadent bonbons as our stomachs could hold.

Being with Julia, I realized the delight of such a moment was the same whether we were dining on second-rate chocolates or full English breakfasts. These two moments carried the same weight in value because of the gift of being close to someone I loved. I would give anything to have one more Christmas morning with my mother and our little soaps and box of chocolate. Oh how I would love to hear her ethereal, lilting laughter one more time.

Since that wasn't possible, I felt as if God were giving me a special gift on this Christmas Eve morning. He gave me breakfast in bed with my niece.

I finished the last sip of cooled tea in my china teacup and whispered a secret thank-you to Gracious God, who always seemed close whenever I was in this room.

Julia watched me drain the last drop. "Good. Now may we pleeeease go downstairs and see the beautiful tree?"

I laughed at her tenacity. "Yes, let's go see the most beautiful tree in the whole, wide world."

I took her hand as we headed down the ornate staircase. I hoped Margaret was staying in the rooms she occupied in the east wing of the manor. I knew from previous visits that she didn't usually wander far from her quarters.

What bothered me was that this was Margaret's home, and in that respect, I was her guest. The last thing I wanted to do was cause this glad time of celebrating to be strained or tense for anyone under this roof. Unfortunately, from past experience I knew that tension was the unnamed ambiance whenever Margaret and I were present in the same room.

Chapter Sixteen

or a day that began so leisurely, everything stepped up its pace as soon as Julia and I went downstairs. Ellie was busy in the kitchen alongside Natasha preparing all sorts of wonderful Christmas feast goodies. She had presents yet to wrap, as did I, and she wanted to pull together a meal for Katharine, who had gone back to the hospital to be with Andrew for the day.

I took in all the details, prepared to help out any way I could, and felt a slight sort of guilt for playing the princess for so long that morning. Ellie didn't mind. She was floating along on her usual river of grace.

"Julia said you heard from Ian. Is that right?" I reached for one of the grapes in a beautiful glass bowl on the marble countertop in Ellie's renovated kitchen.

"Yes! Oh, did you not get that message? We're to keep you occupied today until he's ready."

"Ready for what?"

Julia giggled and covered her mouth. Ellie stopped chopping celery and froze as if she had forgotten something. Or maybe she was trying to remember something.

"We're to keep you occupied until he's ready for Christmas," Ellie said brightly. "That's it. You can imagine how his plans have been upset, what with the unexpected news of Andrew and the visits to hospital, not to mention the last-minute role he played as Father Christmas last night. He has a few things to do today."

"Okay."

I wasn't worried about Ian's readjusted schedule even though Ellie seemed flustered. I knew I would see Ian soon, and that was all that mattered.

Tugging on my hand, Julia said, "May we go now to see the Christmas tree, please?"

"Yes, let's go. Then I'll wrap gifts for your mom."

The largest room in the Whitcombes' beautiful home was referred to as the drawing room. Located at the front of the manor, it boasted the largest windows in the home, with a magnificent view of the tall, ancient trees that stood guard around the circular driveway.

Ellie loved to decorate and had gone all out again this year with her snowflake theme, incorporating touches of sparkly, dangling snowflakes hung from the ceiling on fishing wire. Swags of greenery were looped over the mantel of the enormous fireplace as well as across the doorframe and the front windows. Tiny white lights were woven into each garland. On this gray day, the lights twinkled cheerfully and made the room merry and bright.

The ceilings were high, so Julia's eager voice echoed in the large, open area as she said, "Do you see it? Do you see how big it is? It's the best Christmas tree ever, and we get to have it every year."

"It *is* the best Christmas tree ever." I drew close and stood beside her to admire the commanding beauty of the artificial wonder where it stood in front of the center window. "It's the most wonderful Christmas tree in all the world!"

"I know. I told you it was."

The tree reached at least ten feet, with the lit star at the top adding another foot of dazzle. The white lights that circled the tree were accompanied by a delightful assortment of every type of ornament and dangling prettiness Ellie had collected over the years. Around the base were a dozen or so gifts. More gifts for the children had been clustered around the tree the day before, but at least a dozen of those presents were now cheering up the children in the hospital. Even with those generously offered gifts gone, the Whitcombe children would have an abundant and merry Christmas.

I thought of all the times over the years when I had heard people say Christmas was too commercial and materialistic. They were right, of course. I couldn't disagree. But if any one of those bah-humbug, Christmas Scrooges had lived my life, if they had come from where I came from, with motel soaps and shampoos and never a Christmas tree to fill a room with cheer and wonder, I think they would have softened their railings. If they could feel what I felt at this moment, gazing at the Christmas tree with wide-eyed Julia, they would say that tradition, decorations, and gifts were a beautiful way to celebrate Christ's birth.

"We'd better get to work on those few things your mother asked me to do," I said.

Julia was happy to help. She stayed close most of the day while Mark seemed to find things to do that didn't fall into the chore category. The house hummed with merry-making activity. The kitchen exhaled a stream of wonderful fragrances. Christmas music floated through the house. The lineup of tunes included everything from "I'm Dreaming of a White Christmas" to a variety of boys' choir canticles sung as Mark had sung them, in soul-stirring Latin.

Edward kept to his desk in the library most of the day, but his door remained open. I was aware that Mark and Julia regularly ran in and out to tell their dad this or that about the activities.

At one point in the late afternoon, as I walked past the library on my way to the drawing room with freshly wrapped presents in my arms, I paused by the open door and smiled at Edward. He smiled at me. I could picture my father seated behind that desk and wondered if this home was filled with the same warmth and happiness when Sir James was the head of the household.

I found my opinion of Edward elevating. He was available to his children. They had free access to come into his presence at any time.

Gazing past the library down the long hall that led to Margaret's quarters, I wondered what it would take for Margaret to open her door to me. If that door ever did open, would it remain open?

After the final gifts were deposited under the tree, I returned to the kitchen and admired the assortment of wonderful foods spread across the counter. In one corner Ellie had placed two large wicker picnic hampers. The tops were open, and she was filling them with freshly baked breads, wedges of imported cheese, and a big, fat, wrapped-up ham.

"That's quite a lot of food for Katharine," I observed. "What a feast!"

Ellie jumped and nearly dropped the ham.

"Oh, I didn't see you come in; you startled me. Yes, so, how is everything going with the gift wrapping?"

"It's all finished. The gifts are under the tree. Julia and Mark are both upstairs, and I was about to clean up the mess I made in the dining room with all the wrapping paper."

"Oh, don't fuss with that. It's almost time for you to go. You should get ready."

"Go where?"

"With Ian. He's coming by to pick you up. Did Julia not tell you? Oh, me-me-me, oh my. I knew I should have told you myself."

"That's okay. I should have put my cell phone in my pocket so he could call me. Did he say where we're going?"

Ellie tilted her head like a little bird and looked at me strangely, as if my question were an odd one.

"I'm trying to decide what to wear," I went on. "If we're going out to a nice place for dinner, I don't want to be in jeans when he arrives."

"Oh, yes. Of course. I would say..." Ellie made a funny humming sound as she pursed her lips together and thought. "Something lovely would best fit the occasion, but it should be something comfortable that you love to wear. I think the red dress you wore last night would be perfect for an encore performance."

"Are you sure?"

"Oh, yes! Because you can wear it with the black cashmere sweater, and it will look absolutely elegant."

"I don't have a black cashmere sweater."

Ellie slapped her hand over her mouth. "Oh me. Me-me-me. I certainly am atwitter! I can barely remember what I'm supposed to say and not supposed to say. Come. Come, come, come!"

Ellie wiped her hands on her apron and propelled her short legs at an impressive pace out of the kitchen and into the drawing room. I kept up with her, and when we stopped in front of the tree, she looked around at all the gift boxes that had been rearranged by Julia.

"This one." She reached for a rectangular box tied with a wide, silver ribbon. "Open it now. It's okay. You'll see."

I hugged Ellie before I tore off the wrapping. "Thank you for the cashmere sweater."

She feigned surprise and blinked her eyes. "Why, Miranda! How ever did you guess what I was giving you this year?"

"I'll open it upstairs," I said. "Just so the children don't think I've started something they would like to finish."

"Good idea. And if it doesn't fit, or if you don't like it, it's not a problem to return or exchange. Although, we won't be able to do so today since Ian will be here in fifteen minutes. You really should get going, Miranda!"

I smiled at my willy-nilly sister-in-law and dashed up the stairs. Behind my closed door, I opened the box and pulled out a beautiful—and I was sure very expensive—black cashmere sweater. The fitted, classic sweater went perfectly with the cheery-cherry-merry red dress and made me feel elegant. It transformed and completed the outfit.

I added my fun sparkly necklace and earrings. They weren't expensive, but they added a final glimmery touch, and since I hadn't worn them last night, it felt as if I really were wearing a different outfit.

I didn't have enough time to pay extra attention to my hair, but Ian said he liked it when I wore it down so that it skimmed my shoulders and could easily be, as he said, "tussled by the breeze."

I tried not to think about the obvious fact that everyone else seemed to know this was going to be a "special" evening with Ian. I knew what that meant. How could I not see all the clues?

A little coaching seemed in order so I told myself, *Whatever you do, Miranda, when he pulls out "the box," try to act surprised.*

When I heard loud voices downstairs echoing up the stairway, I knew Ian had arrived. With one last look in the mirror, I thought of how much this felt like a long-buried, youthful wish that never had come true. I never had gone to a high school prom or even a dance where I dressed up and made a grand entrance.

The day had begun with my playing the princess role, and so it continued as I opened my guest room door and promenaded down the fantastic staircase. I was just at the window seat in the landing when Ian came into view in the wide entryway. He was flanked by Mark, Julia, Edward, Ellie, and . . .

Oh, Ian!

He was wearing his dress kilt.

Chapter Seventeen

here she is!" Julia announced my descent with a happy squeal.

All eyes were on me as I carefully made my way down the polished wood stairs. The only eyes I cared about were Ian's, and his eyes definitely were shining with all the affection and admiration a woman could ever dream of receiving.

He placed his hands behind his back and stood tall, as if he were ready for me to inspect him in his formal white shirt, bow tie, jacket, MacGregor plaid kilt, and knee socks held up by elastic bands that we had found in a shop last summer in Windsor.

I smiled my immense approval, and he smiled back the same. Offering me his arm, Ian said, "See you later" to our small audience and led me to the front door.

"Your coat, Miranda!" Ellie rushed to hand me my coat. "I put it in the pocket, just in case."

"Okay," I said, having no idea what she was talking about.

Ian helped me with my coat, and we stepped out the front door under the motto for the Whitcombe manor that was engraved over the entrance, "Grace and Peace Reside Here."

I slipped my hand in the coat pocket and smiled. Ellie had put a handkerchief into my pocket. That was her "just in case" gift. I knew it wasn't just any handkerchief. As I fingered the edges, I could tell it was one of Margaret's handkerchiefs, with her defining touch of a tiny pink rosebud she embroidered in the corner.

I felt squeamish about having one of Margaret's hankies with me. Ellie was free with her gifts for others, but Margaret only gave her embroidered handkerchiefs to those who were closest to her. On several occasions during the past year, Margaret had opportunities to give me one of her unique works of art, but she hadn't done so. What would she think if she knew Ellie had given me one of the rosebud hankies?

Then it occurred to me how much time I spent fretting over what Margaret thought of me. Margaret wasn't coming with us this evening. This was my time to be with Ian. I turned all my focus on him.

Ian opened the car door for me and there, waiting on my seat, was a single red rosebud. The deep merlot fragrance tickled my nose as I gave the rose a twirl across my lips. Apparently the pink rosebud on the edge of the handkerchief wasn't the only rose that would lace this enchanting evening.

"Thank you." I looked into Ian's set expression.

He took my face in his hands and kissed me tenderly on the lips. We shared another kiss before Ian got in the driver's side and headed around the circular driveway and through the open gated entrance.

"How's your dad doing?" I still twirled the rosebud and drew in the scent.

"Much improved."

"That's good news. Katharine must be relieved."

"That she is."

"So, will he be able to come home for Christmas?"

"Yes, definitely."

"Do we need to help Katharine get him at the hospital?"

"Not at the moment."

The car rumbled down the familiar country lane, and I looked at Ian. He was being unusually brief with his answers. But he looked happy. I had the feeling that, in the same way I had put away thoughts of Margaret for our evening together, Ian was setting aside the concerns he had over his dad.

This was our time at last. A contented smile settled on my lips.

The car ambled along, and the slowly setting sun peeked out from behind the gray clouds for the first time that day. As if elated for the chance to finally break through the gloom, the sun shot stunning beams of light that pierced the dormant winter landscape like shafts of translucent hope.

We drove past a row of narrow birch trees lining the road, and the determined sunlight played a flitting game of hide-and-seek between the birches. Elongated strips of light and dark flashed across the lane, producing a strobe light effect. Ian cut through the pulsating lines of sun and shadow and came into an open place in the road where he stopped and let the car roar a moment before making a turn.

We were fully in the sunlight for the briefest of moments, and then the precocious ball of waning fire found her way into the pocket of a waiting woolen cloud. In that brief, sunlit moment, I looked at Ian and smiled. I saw flecks of winter gold reflected in his eyes.

"You're glowing," he said to me.

I could imagine how the slipping sunlight behind me had cast one last fling of radiant amber lights to the ends of my tussled hair.

God, in all His glory, seemed to have sent His golden blessing to lightly touch us both in the closing of the day.

Ian smiled. I smiled back. Then he turned left.

I expected him to turn right. The high road was the most direct way to reach any one of the neighboring towns that had restaurants that would be open on Christmas Eve. Nothing in Carlton Heath would be open.

"Where are we going?"

Ian only smiled.

His low-to-the-ground sports car bumped along the road, and I contented myself to settle into his secret. Maybe we were going to the train station. I kept watch out the window in the twilight to get a glimpse of the Forgotten Rose Cottage.

I felt a wave of the same sadness I had felt the day before when I had realized someone else had stepped up to that small dream of mine and taken the Forgotten Rose Cottage for his own.

The first time I had seen the cottage was last Christmas. I had walked past it on my way to find the Tea Cosy and had noted that it appeared no one lived there.

A few days later, after I had met Ian, the two of us went for a stroll. I was about to return to San Francisco, and the time had come for us to talk about where our relationship might be headed. We were walking past the cottage when Ian stopped, squared his shoulders, and said, "I don't think we're done yet, Miranda." His simple declaration began to topple the fortress that had long protected my untrusting heart.

My response to him that day had been, "I don't think we are either."

Then we kissed for the first time. It was the most natural, mutual, perfectly timed and perfectly executed kiss ever. When I opened my eyes, there was Ian's strong and handsome face. And in the background, behind Ian, was the stone cottage.

That image seared itself into my heart and mind and had kept me hoping and dreaming for the past year.

Resolving not to be sad about the Forgotten Rose Cottage as we approached, I saw a warm, amber light glowing from the two front windows. Curls of smoke rose from the chimney. The front walkway was lined with lanterns on shepherd's hooks just like the ones that lined the entrance to Grey Hall.

The revived cottage looked like something from a fairy tale.

A small "oh" escaped from my lips. Forgotten Rose Cottage looked exactly as I had dreamed it could look. In my fanciful imaginings of what might happen with some strategic renovations to the property, this was what I had seen.

Ian pulled the car to the side of the road and cut the engine.

Memories of our outing at Windsor last summer came back. "Is something wrong with the car?"

"The car is fine. Come with me."

"What's going on?" I asked.

"You'll see."

We walked up the lit pathway past the well-groomed shrubs. I tried to see inside the windows, but they were covered with shades.

"Did someone buy this place and turn it into a restaurant?"

"It's not a restaurant." Ian walked to the front welcome mat and glibly motioned toward the door. Another single red rose was tucked through the ring of the lion's head brass door knocker.

I looked at Ian for an explanation. His face was ruddy. His grin jubilant.

"For you." He handed me the rose. Then reaching for the latch, he said, "And also for you."

He opened the front door of the Forgotten Rose Cottage. "Welcome home, Miranda."

Chapter Eighteen

couldn't move.

"Come." Ian held out his hand to me and invited me over the threshold.

The cottage was lit by firelight and by the flickering amber hope of a dozen votives strategically placed in the sparsely furnished room.

The long stem rose in my hand shook.

"Ian, how...?"

"I'll tell you everything soon enough. Just drink in the moment, Miranda."

In front of us, an earnest stack of logs burned golden in the hearth. The only furniture I saw was a table with four chairs inside the kitchen area and a plush leather loveseat positioned in front of the fire.

On the polished wood floor I noticed a trail of rose petals. As my eyes adjusted to the soft light, I saw that the rose petals led to a Christmas tree in the corner. Ian flipped a light switch by the door, and the tree lit up.

"Ian, it's a Christmas tree!"

"That it is."

"Ian, you got me a Christmas tree."

"That I did."

I followed the rose petal trail to the medium-sized, stout tree. It looked magical in its covering of starry lights. I imagined it had, no doubt, been hewn by Ian and carted here in his convertible. I now understood Ellie's earlier message about Ian not being "ready." The man had been busy today.

As I approached, I noticed something besides the tiny white lights was attached to every branch. And then I saw what it was.

Roses.

Red roses. Dozens and dozens of red rosebuds. They hung like ornaments and nestled in the branches like birds' nests.

The sight was beautiful beyond words. I stood, stared, blinked, and cried a little as I tried to take it in.

"Did you do all this?"

"I had a little help from Katharine."

Ian knew I never had had a Christmas tree. My mother and I never had one. Doralee didn't believe in them. And once I was on my own in an apartment, it seemed silly to pay for a tree when I had no ornaments to decorate it. To the occasional friend or office associate who visited me at Christmastime and remarked about the absence of a tree, I always said I was doing my part to help the environment.

When Ian had found out last Christmas that I never had put up a tree, he said, "One day you'll have your tree, and it will bloom in roses just for you."

At the time, I had thought he was trying to unveil to me his poetic side. I had no idea this romantic man of mine was making plans. Plans that were being unfurled tonight. This was my Christmas tree, and it was covered with roses.

Ian wrapped his arms around me and kissed the side of my neck. "You are my rose, Miranda. And you are forgotten no more."

My tears fell lightly on his arms as he held me secure.

"And this place is no longer 'Forgotten Rose Cottage.' We'll give it a new name." He kissed my shoulder and then my neck. I drew in the fragrant scent of the evergreen tree.

"Ian, I can't believe all this."

"Believe it."

"How did you...?"

"Come and sit." He led me to the loveseat.

"Explain all this to me," I said.

"The cottage is yours, Miranda."

"How? Did you buy it?"

"No."

"Then who? How...?"

Ian got up, walked to the fire, and placed another log on the stack. Leaning against the mantel, he said, "Your father bought the cottage twelve years ago."

"My father?"

"Yes. Sir James, I've been told, was as taken with the property as you were when you first saw it. He bought it without many people knowing because he wanted to use it as his painting studio. That's his table in the kitchen, and the sofa you're sitting on was his as well."

My hand instantly went to the dark brown leather and smoothed over the surface. *My father sat here by this fire. This was his cottage.*

"I knew how much you loved this place, so I made some inquiries last August. When I found out it belonged to Sir James, I went to Edward to see if I might either purchase the property from the estate or lease it from him. He deliberated for some time with the barristers. Last week, at Edward's request and by his hand, the papers were drawn up to give the property to you as part of your inheritance."

My jaw went slack.

"The cottage is yours."

"If Edward did that, it means he had to tell the lawyers who I am."

Ian nodded.

"Did Margaret agree to all this?"

"As far as she needed to for Edward to make the arrangements."

I leaned back and let the implication of this news sink in. Margaret might not approve of me, but Edward agreed to this. He acknowledged the blood relationship between us.

"Edward has papers for you to sign, of course, and there will be time for meetings with the barristers next week to settle all the fine points. The place needs fixing up, but it's yours."

"I can't believe this."

"Believe it. It's true."

The dancing flames in the hearth warmed the smoky, sand-colored stones of the fireplace. Above, on the thick, carved wood mantel, my eye went to a single, long-stemmed red rose that lay rested on the wood beam. Next to the rose was a box. A familiar little white box.

I tried to hide my delight, but the discovery must have

shone in my eyes because Ian cleared his throat and shifted his position.

None of the clever lines that flitted through my thoughts came to rest on my lips. I wanted to tease him, but this didn't seem the moment for that. I would wait for Ian to speak. My answer was ready, as I'm sure he already knew.

"Miranda." Ian gathered up the box and the rose and moved closer to me.

I felt my pulse beat faster.

"You know my heart toward you. It has not wavered from the first. I have set my affections on you and you alone."

Holding out the rose to me, Ian lowered to one knee and took my hand in his. With his soft hazel-brown eyes fixed on mine, he dipped his chin. "Miranda, will you have me for your husband?"

I heard the answer in my heart before it danced off my lips. "Yes. With all my heart, yes."

Ian took the ring from the box and slipped it on my finger. The dainty, platinum ring bumped over my knuckle and settled in its new home. I held out my hand and blinked back the tears.

"The ring belonged to my mother," he said.

"It's beautiful."

"Do you like it, then?"

"I love it." The firelight twinkled in the simple, classic setting. "If I were to pick out a ring, this is what I would have chosen."

Ian settled in beside me and told me how his father, as a young man, had saved his money for years before he could buy

Ian's mother this beautiful ring. "When they married she had a simple, thin band, but my dad always wanted her to have a diamond. When I was a boy, I remember him telling her that every time she looked at the ring she was to remember that she was of great value to him and deeply loved."

I held my hand closer and admired the sparkling diamond and the simple curves of the setting.

"Before my mom died, she took off the ring and gave it to me. She told me to save it because she was sure one day I would meet the right woman. And when I did, she said this ring would whisper to that woman that she is of great value to me and that I loved her deeply."

We drew close for a lingering kiss, and then we kissed again.

"I love you," I whispered.

"And I love you."

Ian drew back. "So, the next question is, when?"

"When what?"

"When will you make good on your promise to marry me?"

"Soon."

"Yes, but when?"

"I was thinking springtime might be nice. It would be pretty here then, wouldn't it? We could have our reception in the garden."

"It might rain, but we know how to adapt to a little rain."

"I would like the service to be at the old church in Carlton Heath."

"Of course."

"In front of the stained glass window."

"Whatever you wish."

"And I'd like to move to Carlton Heath before the spring. The sooner the better."

"It's your home."

"It's our home," I said. "This will be our home."

I had no words after that. Only a few slow tears and a full heart.

Resting my head on Ian's shoulder, I looked at the fire and then closed my eyes. I thought I should say something. Nothing came. Only peace. A deep, abiding peace.

We kissed again, and Ian murmured in my ear, "Are you sure you want to wait all the way until spring? What if I went out and found us an agreeable minister and brought him back here this evening?"

I laughed. "On Christmas Eve?"

Before Ian could press his idea of hunting down a minister, we heard noise coming from outside. It seemed to be coming from the walkway.

"Were you expecting someone?" I asked.

"Ahh!" Ian checked his watch. "They're early. I should have guessed they would be early."

"Who's early?"

Just then we heard the clear, true notes of Mark and Julia's voices as they began singing on our doorstep.

"It's our Christmas Eve supper via special delivery," Ian said. "And from the sounds of it, I'm guessing it's our evening entertainment as well."

Chapter Nineteen

ogether Ian and I went to the front door to welcome the Whitcombe family. Ellie and Edward were each holding one of the beautifully decorated picnic hampers I had seen Ellie filling earlier in her kitchen. Julia jitter-wiggled her way right over the threshold and wrapped her arms around my middle.

"Did you know?" Julia asked. "I tried very hard to keep the secret, but Mummy said you might have guessed."

"No, I didn't guess a thing about the cottage." I looked up at Edward with an intense gaze of gratitude and said, "Thank you, Edward. Thank you so much."

"What about the tree?" Julia asked. "Aunt Katharine told me about the tree, but she said I mustn't tell. Do you like it?"

"Yes. Very, very much."

"What about the proposal?" Ellie asked. Then opening her eyes wide and slapping her hand over her mouth, she said in a small voice, "He has asked you already, hasn't he? We did give you enough time, Ian, did we not?"

"Plenty of time." Ian took the heavy basket from Ellie. "I asked her, and she said yes. There's not much to tell."

I swatted playfully at his arm for the way he had so quickly downplayed the intensely emotional last thirty minutes of our lives.

"Of course she said yes." Ellie gave me a hug and reached for my hand to see the beautiful ring.

Everyone admired it appropriately, and Ellie said, "Did you need the hanky?"

I realized everything had happened so fast that I hadn't thought to reach for the hanky. I also realized I still had on my coat. Unfastening the clasps, I removed my coat and slipped into the role of hostess of the "No Longer Forgotten Rose Cottage."

I said, "May I take your coats?"

"We might have hangers in the bedroom closet," Ian said. "I haven't checked."

I gathered all the coats the way Ellie had in the cloakroom at Grey Hall and went to the back of the cottage to the bedroom. It was empty except for two blank canvases propped against the wall and a collapsed easel beside them.

My father's unfinished paintings.

In a way, I was also one of his unfinished paintings. The canvas of my life and Ian's from here on out were blank and ready to be painted. This was a place of new beginnings for us.

The closet was empty and void of hangers, so I stacked the coats on the floor and turned to join the others. However, Mark had stepped into the bedroom and was standing nearby as if he had something to say.

"I wanted you to know that I did what you said." Mark looked solemn.

I wasn't sure what he meant.

"I told my grandmother what I had overheard her saying to my father about you."

"Oh. Good. That was good, Mark. What did she say?"

"She was not pleased, I will tell you that. She said I should keep the information to myself."

I nodded my agreement.

"I thought you should know."

"Thank you, Mark." I smiled at him, hoping to put him more at ease. "You did the right thing."

"You did the right thing as well." He was sounding awfully mature. "I was glad you told me the truth. I'm not as young as they all think I am. I know much more than they think I do."

"What about also telling your parents? I think they would like to know what you heard and what you know at this point."

"I don't think my parents would understand."

"You might be surprised. Talking to them would be a good thing for all of you."

I knew Ellie and Edward would appreciate the gift of their teenage son opening up to them. He had gone to Margaret on his own. Perhaps the rest would come without my nudging.

I put my hand on Mark's shoulder and said in my most sincere voice, "I love you, Mark. I want you to know that."

"I know." He looked away.

Without prolonging the moment, I said, "Good. Now let's go see what your mom brought in those baskets."

Mark and I joined the others as Ellie finished laying out

her abundant Christmas Eve dinner spread. She had thought of everything for our picnic by the fire. We had sliced cold ham and four different sorts of cheese with stone-ground wheat bread. The gourmet assortment of mustards, pickles, and olives gave us an exceptional variety to choose from. There also was a creamy pasta salad with peas.

I had just finished helping Ellie put out an assortment of little cakes when she instructed everyone on where to begin with all the goodies. She had spread out a blanket for the children to sit on the floor since the number of seats was limited.

Out of the corner of my eye, I caught Mark's disgruntled acceptance of his being one of the "children" who would have to sit on the lowly blanket.

I didn't think it would be humanly possible to feel any happier than I did at that moment. The only person missing was Margaret. I concluded that her absence was her choice and an indication of how things would be from here on out. Some things might not be mendable. I had every piece of the family puzzle except the Margaret piece.

I focused back on the moment and the circle of people who were making this Christmas Eve picnic a festive celebration of our engagement. The laughter and words of praise for Ellie's culinary delights were punctuated by a subtle vibrating sound followed by a beep. The source of the buzz and bing was Edward's cell phone.

He ignored it each time, but due to the frequency of the prompts, Ellie finally said, "You really should have a listen. It could be something amiss with your mother."

Edward stepped into the vacant bedroom while the rest of

us carried on our merriment. A moment later he returned to the living room with a grave expression on his face. Everyone looked at him, waiting for an explanation. All he did was motion for me to join him in the other room.

"Is everything okay?" I asked, once we were around the corner from the others.

"I thought you should see this." Edward held out his phone so I could view the picture displayed on the small screen.

I squinted until the image became clear.

All the air seemed to siphon out of the room. My hand went to my mouth as I whispered, "Oh no."

Chapter Twenty

s that me?" I asked Edward, hoping it wasn't but knowing it was. "Is that a picture of me?"

"Apparently it is. Can you read the headlines?"

"Yes."

"This hit the newsstands in London an hour ago."

"How did the press find out? How did they get my picture?"

"I thought you might be able to tell me."

I shook my head and felt my fingers go numb.

Ian stepped into the room just then, and reading the expression on my face, he came to my side. "What's happened? What is it?"

Edward showed him the picture. I was facing the camera, but I had no particular expression.

"I can't make out the headline," Ian said.

In an emotionless voice, Edward repeated the news line header. " 'Sir James Had a Love Child.' "

Ian ran his fingers through his hair. "We have to quench this before it goes any further."

"It's already on the Internet," Edward said. "And syndicated press. My assistant has been monitoring the situation. Miranda, who knows about your identity? Who do you think might have leaked this?"

Mark was the first person who came to mind. Mark was upset, true, but he was only thirteen. He wouldn't release such information to the press. Or would he?

Then I remembered who else knew. And so did Ian.

He punched his right fist into the palm of his left hand. "It was your old boyfriend, wasn't it? He sold you out to the tabloids."

"I can't imagine Josh would do that." I looked at the picture again on Edward's phone, trying to make out the background to understand where I had been when the picture was taken. "That's the sweater I wore when I arrived in London. So it is a recent photo."

I looked up at Ian. "I don't want to believe it was Josh, but..."

"Where's your phone?" Ian asked. "You have his number, don't you? Is he still in London?"

"I don't know. I think I have his card in my coat pocket but—"

Ian was across the room in one swift motion. He pulled out Josh's business card and punched the number into my phone.

I rubbed the tightening muscles on the back of my neck. "If that's his business number, he probably won't be there since it's Christmas Eve."

Ian couldn't hear me, so he held the phone to the side of his ear with the screen facing me. When he turned the phone that way, an instant memory came back to me.

"Paddington station," I said. "The guy at Paddington station who offered me his seat. He's the one who took the photo of me. He took it with his cell phone."

"Are you sure?" Ian asked.

"I'm pretty sure. It makes sense. The man was close enough to overhear me talking to Josh. When he offered me a seat, it seemed a little odd, but I didn't think much of it at the time."

"Let me understand this." Edward's expression stiffened. "You're saying you told a stranger at Paddington your connection to us?"

"No. Josh isn't a stranger. He's my old boyfriend. A number of years ago I showed Josh the Father Christmas photograph with you and your dad... I mean, our dad...." I felt awkward changing the words to "our dad," but that was the truth.

Ian closed my phone, disconnecting the call to Josh.

"I didn't expect to see Josh at Paddington. It was a coincidence, and it just seemed right to tell him why I was here since..."

Ian took up my defense. "Josh was the one who urged Miranda to come to Carlton Heath in the first place."

"That's right. And he's a professional counselor, so I would like to think I can trust him to maintain confidentiality. I didn't think anyone could hear me when I was talking to him; it was so noisy at the station. But then this man got up from the bench behind us and held his cell phone the way Ian just did, and I think he took my picture with his phone."

"Well then, that's it." Edward reached for his phone and pressed some numbers. "I have calls to make."

I felt my chest compress. I suddenly understood much more clearly why Margaret and Edward had appeared so devastated last Christmas when I had revealed my identity to them. As a family, they had finally experienced a short break from all the media attention after Sir James passed away. My appearance meant it was only a matter of time before they ceased being a private family once more. And now that day had come.

I felt sick to my stomach about it all. "I wish this hadn't happened."

"Well, it has," Ian said in a comforting voice. "So we go on from here."

Edward's demeanor was as reserved and steady as ever as he finished his phone call and turned to Ian and me with direction. "I've conferred with our legal counsel. We had a plan in place for when this might happen. I've made the necessary calls, and now all the steps will be put in motion."

"What steps exactly?" I asked.

"We've put out a call for a press conference the day after tomorrow. Better to air our side of the story on Boxing Day than on Christmas. I can assist you in preparing your remarks. I will go on camera, but Mother will not."

"Wait, Edward. I'm not following you. What do you mean a press conference? Aren't we trying to avoid the press?"

"We have a system. This was routine when my father was alive. The press wants a story. We want peace and quiet. If we don't give them a story, they create their own. Therefore, we control the story through our network of publicists and reporters. All you'll need to do is go on camera for thirty seconds, ninety at the most. You'll deliver a prepared statement. It's best if you can do it without notes."

I felt as if the room had tilted. Ian put his strong arm around me.

Edward looked at his watch. "I've alerted our security service. They'll be at the gate when we return to the house tonight in case the paparazzi are waiting. It would be best if you rode back with us rather than in Ian's car."

"Edward, I'm so, so sorry."

"We all supposed this day would come," Edward said matter-of-factly.

"I just hate that it did," I said. "I don't like thinking about what this will do to Margaret. It's going to change what everyone thinks of her and what they think of Sir James."

Edward looked at me with what could almost be considered a softening in his expression. "Miranda, this is going to change how people view you as well. Have you thought about that?"

No, I hadn't thought about that. My eyes welled with tears, but I refused to let them fall.

Ian drew me close. "Calm yourself, Miranda. We'll work this out together."

Edward exited the room. I could hear him giving an abbreviated summary to the adults in the other room. When Ian and I entered, I noticed that Ellie had taken Julia into the kitchen to distract her young ears.

Mark, however, sat with the adults. "You needn't speak in code, Father. I already know."

I couldn't tell if Mark's announcement startled Edward. What I did know was that Mark was trying his best to prove his place as an adult in the Whitcombe clan.

I knew I would do well to follow his example and be brave.

Chapter Twenty-one

As Edward predicted, a gathering of photographers awaited us as the town car with its darkened windows rolled up to the front gate of the Whitcombe manor. In all the times I'd come and gone from the house, I never had seen the gate closed or the security booth manned, which it was tonight.

"This is how it used to be," Mark said to me.

Ellie, in her eternally effervescent optimism, said, "Do you remember that, Markie? You liked the guard at the back garden post. What was his name? He had the big dog with the white spot on its nose."

"Raymond," Mark said. "The guard was Raymond, and his dog was Digger."

"That's right. Perhaps Raymond and Digger will be back at their post."

I tried to imagine how Ellie had carved out such a successful marriage and journeyed through motherhood with guards, dogs, and paparazzi as part of the everyday schedule.

We rolled through the open gate, and cameras flashed against the car's darkened windows. I looked down, just in case the cameras captured an image in spite of the shades. Edward and Ellie didn't flinch. They seemed confident in their anonymity inside the specially prepared car.

"You'll want to use this." Edward pulled a large, black umbrella out from under the seat. "With such advancements in telescopic lenses, it's best to exit with the umbrella between yourself and the front gate."

I followed Edward's instructions and opened the huge umbrella once I was outside the car and then used it as a covering for the six or so feet I crossed to the front door. The rest of the family used umbrellas as well and entered behind me. A tall man dressed all in black with a cord hanging from his right ear greeted me in the entryway and took the umbrella from me.

"Subject is clear," he said to whomever was at the other end of his sophisticated communication system.

I wasn't quite sure what to do, so I thanked him and looked to Edward for direction. This was all different from how things had been at the house a few hours ago. Yet Ellie and Edward acted as if the presence of all these people in their home were normal.

Edward was carrying a sleeping Julia in his arms. Ellie was ushering Mark forward. Ian was the last to enter. Behind him I could see the faint flash of cameras like distant lightning.

"Off to bed with you, Mark," Ellie said. "We have an early morning! When you wake up, it will be Christmas."

Mark looked sullen. He wasn't to be tempted off to bed with the promise of new toys in the morning. His serious, adult leanings were in full play tonight.

"I think I should be allowed to sit in on your meeting, Mum and Dad."

Edward and Ellie exchanged glances.

"I heard you, Father, when you were talking on the phone with Grandmother before we left the cottage. You said you plan to talk with everyone tonight. I should like to be included."

"All right then, Mark. You may sit with us. Let me put your sister into bed first. Ian, would you start a fire for us in the drawing room?"

"I can start the fire, Father." Mark spoke with a stubborn edge to his voice.

"That would be lovely, Mark," Ellie said, taking over directions for Edward. "While you and Uncle Ian start the fire, Miranda and I will get a pot of tea brewing."

I followed Ellie into the kitchen while Ian trailed Mark into the drawing room.

"How do you do this, Ellie?"

"Do what?"

"This life you guys have. Everyone is taking this alert status so calmly. I feel horrible that Edward had to call in security on Christmas Eve, of all nights. These men should be home with their families."

"They'll be home for Christmas. Edward has a sophisticated rotation plan. It's not as bad as it might seem. For any of us. We're used to it, Miranda. You'll get used to it too. Life will go back to normal quickly. You'll see. Today's news is always tomorrow's liner for the canary cage. That's what Sir James used to say."

Ellie put the teakettle on the stove and looked around the

clean kitchen. "Natasha did a lovely job cleaning up. I'm afraid I left her with quite a mess."

Glancing at me in my still unconvinced slump, she continued her cheer-up talk. "Now, don't worry, Miranda. This will blow over. These media explosions always do. It may seem like a mess now, but it will settle. You'll be old news before you know it."

Lowering myself onto one of the stools at the counter, I said, "I still want to apologize."

"For what?"

"For the inconvenience this breaking news is to you and your family, but especially to Margaret."

"You could always tell her that, couldn't you? I mean, it wouldn't hurt to say such things to her at this point. You're saying them from your heart, and that does make all the difference, doesn't it?"

I nodded, but instead of making an effort to face Margaret, I lingered in the kitchen. My excuse was that Ellie needed help to prepare a tea tray with six china teacups and saucers. We used the same silver tray from which Julia and I had been served our princess breakfast in bed. I had a feeling that this tea party would be anything but cozy and giggly, though.

Ellie carried the tray to the drawing room while I followed with another tray laden with grapes, cheese, cookies, and cream and sugar for the tea.

The long, low coffee table that sat in the center of the circled seating area was decorated with a small nativity scene in the middle. I remembered seeing the hand-carved figurines in Ellie's kitchen window last Christmas.

We lowered the two trays to either end of the coffee table, leaving the miniature nativity set unruffled in the center.

For some reason, that was important to me. It was, after all, Christmas Eve. Christ's birth, that generous gift to us from Father God, was the center of this holiday celebration. It was in this home a year ago that that truth was made real to me. I needed to know now, even if it was demonstrated in only this subtle way, that the nativity was still the focal point of this night and this home.

Margaret already was seated in the drawing room by the fire, but I avoided making eye contact with her. I was aware that all the window shades were drawn. The lights on the tree were lit, but they didn't seem to cast the same merry twinkle across the room as they had that morning. The furniture had been pulled around in a half circle facing the fire.

"Would everyone like tea then?" Ellie asked as, with expert ease, she poured from the silver teapot. I assisted by passing around the steaming cups of tea balanced on the saucers.

When I handed Margaret her cup, our eyes met for a flicker of a second. "I understand congratulations are in order," she said.

"Yes, thank you," I said.

Ian added, "Miranda agreed to be my wife. In spite of all the uproar, this is a very happy night for us."

"Indeed," Margaret said.

I wished the right words would come to me at that moment and I could say to Margaret what was on my heart. But I froze with a simplistic sort of smile sitting on my lips in a wavy line.

Edward picked up the conversation from there.

"I will start by giving everyone a summary of the current situation."

He went through the list of who had been contacted, where the security was in effect, and what was scheduled for the media interview the day after Christmas.

All of this seemed so un-American to me. Disaster was at our doorstep, and we were settled around a fire, drinking tea, planning our civilized counterattack.

Edward continued. "I was reminded by one of my advisors that this will pass quickly due to some of the other more scandalous happenings in the news at the moment."

I hadn't kept up on British or world news for the past few days, so I wasn't aware of what scandalous happenings were going on, but I did hold onto what Ellie had said in the kitchen about how this bit of news would pass quickly. I knew things would be intense for a few days and probably shaky for the rest of my stay. But then was it possible the big rush of the media would be over?

I hoped so.

As Edward concluded his update, I began to breathe a little more deeply and steadily. I was trying to muster up the courage to say something that would let Margaret know how much I regretted bringing this upon their home, especially at Christmas.

Before I could speak up, Mark said, "May I say something, Father?"

"Yes, Mark."

"A person should not be blamed for something that's not their fault. Isn't that right?"

"Yes." Edward was looking at Mark as if he wasn't sure where the conversation was headed.

"So a person like Aunt Miranda should not be blamed because of who her father was."

An odd hush settled on the gathering. If there was any doubt Mark understood what was going on, that doubt was now removed.

"There are a few more complications, son. It's not as easy as all that."

Margaret shifted in her chair. I had a feeling she was about to get up and leave.

Mark, who had been watching my expression, said, "I did not choose that you would be my father. Aunt Miranda did not choose who would be her father either. None of us can choose who his or her parents will be. Wouldn't you agree, Grandmother?"

Edward jumped in, deflecting the curved question Mark had tossed at Margaret. "We may not have our choice as to how we come in to the Whitcombe clan, Mark, but it is up to each of us how we choose to live with the Whitcombe burdens and blessings."

His statement seemed to settle equally on all of us in the room. My first thought went to how many blessings this family had received. My next thought was that I might very well be the burden each of them would have to bear.

Ian reached over and took my hand, giving it an encouraging squeeze.

"I propose," Edward continued, "the less said on this topic, the better for the time being."

"Right," Ellie agreed. Popping up, she reached for the silver serving tray. "What do you say we all turn in for the night? You know, Mark, we have lots of days ahead of us that we'll be together. We can always talk later, can't we? What if we all get some sleep? What do you say to that?"

Margaret was the first to rise and leave the room. Mark trailed her, with Ellie following him carrying one of the tea trays. Ian, Edward, and I were left by the waning fire.

For a few minutes none of us spoke. Ian was the one to break the silence. "I want you to know, Edward, that I appreciate how you've supported Miranda and me, especially the past few months. You have put a fine and noble effort out there for both of us, and I know your father would be pleased with how you've handled the blessing of being a Whitcombe."

"Not at all." Edward brushed off the comment as he stood up, preparing to leave the room. "I'll keep both of you informed should there be any changes in our plans or schedule. Ellie said she wants to prepare a family brunch for us at around ten o'clock tomorrow morning. We'll see you then, of course."

I looked down at my hands. The light from the fire reflected on my engagement ring and sparked in me a sweet glimmer of hope.

I held onto that glimmer through the night as I slept in the upstairs guest room. My sleep was restless. I would doze off for a few hours and then awaken with a horrible mixture of elation over remembering that Ian and I were engaged, quickly followed by the heaviness that stayed on me after Margaret left the drawing room.

When the filtered morning light finally entered my

chambers, bringing the details of the room into focus, an unexpected, faint signal seemed to go off in my head. The signal was telling me to leave. Run. Jump ship now. Go! Get far away from this place and these people.

Let this be your great closing scene on these relationships, Miranda. Now is your chance to prove how invisible you can be. Quietly gather your belongings right now and leave. No curtain call. Just go.

That's what my mother would have done. I knew where those thoughts were coming from. I knew the ancient fire from which they were forged.

But I was not a mirror image of my mother, just as I was not consciously reflective of my father. I was a unique blend of the two in the innermost parts of my makeup. But mostly I was myself. I was free to make my own decisions.

And my decision was to marry Ian and settle here in Carlton Heath.

Chapter Twenty-two

ue to my restless sleep, I stayed in bed and slept much later than I expected. It was after nine by the time I was up and dressed and on my way downstairs. Last Christmas jet lag had awakened me along with early riser Julia, and the two of us had quietly watched the snow fall.

This year she must have had instructions to leave me to my slumber because I wasn't aware that she had tried to wake me.

Making my way downstairs, I could hear voices coming from the drawing room around the tree. With a determined heart, I put on my best Christmas morning smile and stopped at the open door of the drawing room. Around the tree sat Ellie, Edward, Mark, and Julia. They were opening gifts and taking pictures. None of them noticed I was in the doorway.

I decided to pull back and not enter into their family gift exchange the way I had the previous year. Instead of being with the Whitcombe foursome, I faced what I had been avoiding all last night — that I needed to talk with the matriarch of the family. I needed to tell her from my heart, as Ellie had said, how sorry I was for the situation she was facing.

Since Margaret wasn't with the others around the tree, I assumed she was in her apartments at the end of the hall.

With each step down the long hallway, I felt my heart beat a little faster. I wished Ian were with me, but he was accompanying Katharine to the hospital this morning to take Andrew home. Besides, I knew this was a conversation I needed to have alone with Margaret.

I paused in the middle of the hallway. To the right was a series of small, rectangular windows positioned at eye level. Each window was painted with a small pink rosebud in the center. Margaret had painted the rosebuds, just as she had embroidered the handkerchiefs with rosebuds.

The irony of the symbol that seemed to represent so much to both of us settled on me as I looked out the window into the back garden. Just down the lane was a cottage — my cottage — with a Christmas tree — my Christmas tree — covered in red roses. Margaret and I were both women who had been romanced and loved and who carried with them tender images of the beauty of that love.

I hated being the living, breathing evidence that Sir James had at one moment been unfaithful to his love for Margaret. Yet Mark was so right when he said that wasn't my fault.

Pressing my feet forward toward Margaret's apartments, I tried to rehearse what I would say to her. None of the practice sentences cooperated nicely as I tried to line them up.

Standing for a moment before the closed door, I drew in a

deep breath. I still didn't know what I would say. But I did know that my heart toward Margaret was sympathetic and sincere. My feelings toward our complicated situation were simple. I wanted peace. Peace and grace, just like the motto that was etched over the front door of this home.

My father was the one who put the motto over the door. Peace and Grace Reside Here.

Without realizing it, as I repeated the motto, my hand rose and covered my heart as if I were about to make a pledge. My whispered prayer right before I knocked on Margaret's door was, "May peace and grace reside here, in my heart, as well."

My hand rose and knocked four taps.

"Come." Margaret's voice from behind the door sounded strong.

I pressed open the door and saw her seated in one of the dark red chairs that flanked the fireplace in her spacious apartment. A warm fire glowed in the hearth. Soft Christmas carols played in the background. The window shades were down. A vanilla-scented candle flickered on the round table between the two chairs.

She didn't turn to see who it was, so I asked, "Margaret, would it be all right if I came in?"

"Yes." She still didn't turn to face me.

I never had been inside her quarters. As I approached the fireplace, I saw the morning newspaper on the floor beside her chair. My photo was there—front-page news. Seeing it so boldly displayed made me feel sick to my stomach.

She turned to look at me, and I could see her eyes were red and swollen. I stepped closer. Her stature seemed to diminish by the large chair. Her expression was that of a young child and not that of a fierce matriarch.

My lips seemed to stick together, and my throat felt as if it were swelling shut. The first words that peeped out before I could stop them were, "Margaret, I am so sorry."

Then more words tumbled out from my heart. "I want to apologize to you, Margaret. I've brought complications to your life. I hate that my existence has been a source of pain for you. I realize you have no reason to take me into your home, let alone into your heart. Especially now, with this on the front page of the newspaper and with reporters lining up at the gate. But I have to tell you that all I want is peace between us. Peace and grace."

Margaret motioned for me to sit in the chair across from her in front of the fire. Her gaze was on the fire, not on me. She took a long while before responding. I waited, practicing the same sort of peace and grace toward her that I was asking her to show to me.

When she spoke, it was in a low and weary voice. "I do believe that, if my husband were still here, he would have welcomed you into our home without reservation. He would not have hesitated to show you his love, his approval, and his kindness. He would have expressed great joy today to hear of your engagement."

Her words warmed me. But only for a moment.

"However, my husband is no longer here. And I am not my husband. It is up to me to choose, as my son said, how I will respond to the blessings and burdens that come with being a Whitcombe."

I nodded, waiting for her to continue.

"Mark was right, of course. It's not your fault you were born. Yet..." Lowering her chin, Margaret continued. "I heard something last evening at Grey Hall. I don't think the woman who said it realized I was within hearing distance."

I immediately thought of the way I had spoken too loudly at Paddington station. Was Margaret about to compare my mistake to the way one of the Carlton Heath busybodies had failed to exercise discretion?

Margaret apparently had another objective in mind. "One of the women asked who you were and why you were seated in our row. She wondered if you were a friend of Ellie's. The other woman stated that she had heard that you were the daughter of a homeless, unwed mother and that the Whitcombes had taken you in."

I couldn't argue with the description. It was true.

"Mark followed me to my rooms last evening," Margaret continued. "He was quite set on making his point clear to me. I tried to explain that he did not understand the implications of the scandal of your birth. He sat in that chair where you are sitting now, and he said to me, 'Grandmother, is Christmas not also about a scandalous birth?' I have been thinking on this for most of the night."

"I would never compare my mother with Mary," I said quickly.

"Nor I," Margaret echoed firmly. "Yet a few curious parallels are in play."

"I don't know about that, but I do accept what the woman said at Grey Hall. I am the daughter of an unwed woman, and yes, I think it could be said that she was homeless."

"That may be, Miranda." Margaret looked at me for the first time. "But you are also the daughter of a fine and noble man who had a well-established home. He would have wanted me to receive you as his own. I suppose I have gained an odd sort of sympathy for Joseph in this small drama we seem to be playing out in my home. Joseph chose to enter into the circumstances, as inconvenient as they were. He adopted the Christ child as his."

Once again, I wanted to dismantle the parallels Margaret was drawing between Jesus' family and the Whitcombe family. I didn't think I should be compared to Christ.

But, for some reason, the combination of Mark's words to her and the sympathies she felt toward Mary and Joseph's lives seemed to be the brick and mortar she was using to build a bridge toward me. I was ready to meet her halfway.

Margaret cleared her throat. "You asked a few moments ago if I might extend to you peace. Peace and grace. These are the words my husband had written over the doorpost of this home long ago. He often said those would be the qualities that would mark our family. I regret to say that, with you, I have not remained true to his wish."

With a deep breath, she said, "Miranda, I offer you peace within these walls. You are welcome in this home, in this village, and in this family. I choose to believe that you are not a burden to the Whitcombe family; you are a blessing."

I went to Margaret in one swift motion and offered her my open arms. She responded with surprise at my exuberance. Yet she received my hug, and there was no mistaking the intent of her heart or the intent of mine. Together we were marking a new beginning.

"Thank you," I whispered to her as we drew apart.

"May the Father's grace and peace remain over us," she said as a benediction. I knew she meant our heavenly Father. But for me, in that moment, the term also carried with it the blessing of my birth father.

And that was all I had ever longed for.

Chapter Twenty-three

I left Margaret's quarters a different person. The burden I had carried for the past year of trying to prove myself worthy of acceptance was gone. In its place was a calm assurance. It felt as if the "nativity scene" of my life was now balanced.

I wondered if Margaret had any idea of the immensity of the Christmas gift she had just given me. The week ahead would be one such as I had never experienced. But she had. This was a familiar path for her. Margaret had it within her power to guide me through the deep waters.

For the first time, I believed she would stand beside me through whatever lay ahead.

I was eager to go to the drawing room now, feeling like a different person than the one who had sat at the family meeting in that room the night before.

When I rounded the corner at the end of the long hall and walked into the wide entryway, a rush of cold air filled the open space. The security guard was holding the door as Ian entered with his arm around Andrew. Katharine was right behind them.

I rushed to meet them. Katharine gave me a kiss on my cheek from her chilled lips.

"Look at you!" I said to Andrew. "You're up and going strong. I'm so glad you're here!"

Andrew, the jolly ole elf, caught my eye and raised an eyebrow. He had looked at me that same way a year ago when he had "delivered" Ian to me as the last gift on his Father Christmas rounds. Fixing his expectant expression on mine, he said, "I hear there is news to be told."

"Yes, there is news to be told." I held out my hand. "Very good news."

I looked at Ian, and he winked at me. I winked back.

Returning my gaze to Andrew, I saw a rim of silver tears welled in his eyes.

"You said yes to the man, did ya?" Andrew asked, trying to sound gruff.

"I did."

"And did he go down on his knee?"

"He did."

"Well done." Andrew gave Ian a fatherly nod of approval.

"The ring is beautiful, Andrew. I love it. Thank you." I didn't know exactly what to say for such an extraordinary gift.

"She would have loved you as much as the rest of us." Andrew took my hand to his lips and gave the memory-filled ring a tender kiss. Then he looked up at me with an expression of tender affection.

I started to cry.

I hadn't realized that Margaret had left her apartment and was now part of our gathering in the entryway. Just as I was about to wipe my tears with the back of my hand, I felt a soft hand slip into mine. It was Margaret's. She was handing me a handkerchief. One of her rosebud handkerchiefs.

I looked her in the eye and smiled my appreciation for the small gift with the enormous significance.

The rest of the Whitcombe family joined us in the entryway. Mark looked at his grandmother, and then he looked at me. I made sure he could see that I was holding a pink rosebud handkerchief—Margaret's and my flag of truce. Mark lifted his chin the same way his father often did and gave me a slight nod of acknowledgment that he understood what I was communicating.

Julia wiggled up close to Andrew and was waiting for her chance to say her little hello to him.

"I'm glad you're better now, Uncle Andrew," she said.

"So am I, dear child. So am I."

"Did you see our beautiful Christmas tree? You must come see it." Julia reached for Andrew's hand and tugged for him to come with her to admire it.

"First, we've something important to do."

"What's that?" Julia asked.

"Miranda must make good on her promise and kiss the patient man."

I took two eager steps toward Ian and met his lips, giving him a full kiss. Julia giggled softly.

"What are you doing?" Andrew cried. "I said you were to

kiss the patient man. Have you not heard I was in hospital? I'm the *patient* man here. I meant for you to kiss me!"

Everyone burst out laughing. I made good on my promise. I planted a big kiss on Andrew's cheek.

"That's better. Now, tell me, Ellie, have I come to the right place for some Christmas breakfast? I want to know that I didn't leave the disagreeable porridge of the past few days for nothing."

"Andrew, you came to the right place! I was just about to set out the Christmas buffet. Isn't it wonderful that we're all together? I couldn't be more pleased. It's a gift, isn't it? A lovely blessing. This is going to be the best Christmas ever."

Ian reached his strong arm around my shoulders and drew me close. I had the feeling he was never, ever going to let me go. He pressed his lips to my ear and whispered, "Happy Christmas, Miranda, my rose."

As he heart-meltingly rolled the r's, I leaned in closer and felt my heart filling with the realization that at last I was fully engaged. Not just engaged to Ian. I was engaged to this family. I was a Whitcombe, and soon enough I would become a MacGregor.

The Father of Christmas had once again brought peace on earth. And I was home at last.

Reading Group Guide

1) In this story, the word *engage* takes on many different meanings for Miranda; the most obvious is "engaged to be married." How else is Miranda engaged throughout this story?

2) In the second chapter, Josh says, "I've found that truth has a way of rising to the surface. Sometimes you must wait for the truth to float to the top. Other times you must go to it, take it by the hand, and pull it up with all your might." What do you think he means? Do you agree with his assessment of truth? Look at the discussion between Mark and Miranda on pages 55–58 for more insight. Can you think of a time when truth was revealed in one of these ways in your own life? Briefly describe the experience.

3) Many times in *Engaging Father Christmas*, life doesn't go as planned. List some of these moments in the story. How do you see God's hand working in those moments as the story progresses? Have you ever had moments like this in your life? How was God's plan revealed as time progressed?

Reading Group Guide

4) What do you think Miranda means when she says, "This is the part of Christmas when we can hear heaven and nature sing" (pg. 94)? Miranda thinks about this song phrase a little earlier in the story (pg. 82). Reread this passage. Have you ever had a moment when God seemed as big as He seems to Miranda? Please share this moment with your reading group.

5) In the passage when Mark, Ian, and Miranda stop to enjoy the moon (pgs. 81–83), what words are used to describe the moon? Why do you think the author chose those words? How is this experience a Christmas gift to Mark, Ian, Miranda, and also to God? How do you make a point at Christmastime to give the gift of your worship to God?

6) Mark and Julia's tender love toward the children in the hospital makes a difference in many young lives, including their own. What can you do this Christmas to show God's selfless love to someone in need?

7) Starting on page 99, "Princess Miranda" and "Princess Julia" enjoy breakfast together in bed. This scene reminds Miranda of her early morning Christmas "breakfasts" of chocolates with her mother. Obviously Miranda's childhood Christmas traditions were very different from Julia's. What traditions did you celebrate as a child, and what do you do to celebrate now? How have these traditions given you a sense of identity and belonging?

Reading Group Guide

8) Miranda feels connected to the Forgotten Rose Cottage. How has her life compared with the story of the cottage? Read Jeremiah 29:11–12 and discuss how these verses apply.

9) Sir James was a great artist. He excelled at acting, but he was also interested in painting. On page 126 Miranda discovers her father's unfinished paintings at the Forgotten Rose Cottage. How does Miranda's evaluation of herself as one of her father's unfinished paintings apply to our relationship with Father God, the Master Artist?

10) Miranda's true identity is revealed against her will through circumstances that she has no control over. Even though she and the Whitcombe family wanted to keep the family secret hidden, what good came out of the revelation? What does this tell us about the benefit of unveiling secrets?

11) How does the Christmas story of Jesus' birth play a role in the healing that occurs between Miranda and Margaret? In what ways did this view of His birth affect you?

12) Miranda is much more capable and willing to express love in *Engaging Father Christmas* than she was in *Finding Father Christmas*. What do you think caused this change? How might this apply to your life? Read 1 John 4:7–8.

About the Author

Robin Jones Gunn is the bestselling author of seventy books, representing nearly 4 million copies sold. In 2007 she won the Christy award for excellence in fiction for her novel *Sisterchicks in Gondolas* and was a Christy award finalist for *Wildflowers*. A dozen of her novels have appeared at the top of the CBA bestseller list, including her wildly successful Sisterchicks series, the romantic Glenbrooke series and the popular Christy Miller series for teens. Robin's Women of Faith novel, *Gardenias for Breakfast*, is a favorite for book clubs. Thousands of teens from around the world have written letters to Robin sharing how God used her popular Christy Miller series, Sierra Jensen series, and Katie Weldon series to bring them to Christ as well as lead them to make life-changing decisions regarding purity. Robin and her husband of thirty-one years live near Portland, OR, where they are members of Imago Dei Community along with other Christian authors including Donald Miller, the author of *Blue Like Jazz*. She serves on the board of directors for Jerry B. Jenkins's Christian Writers Guild as well as on the board of directors for Media Associates International. You can learn more about Robin on her Web site at www.robingunn.com.

If you liked
Engaging Father Christmas, you'll love . . .

FINDING

FATHER

CHRISTMAS

"Gunn . . . dishes up a perfect Christmas story about sacrifice, family, and the true meaning of love."   —*Library Journal*

Miranda Carson's desperate search for her father takes a turn she never expected when she finds herself in London a few days before Christmas with only a few feeble clues to who her father might be. Unexpectedly welcomed into a family that doesn't recognize her, and whom she's quickly coming to love, Miranda faces a terrible decision.

Should she reveal her true identity and destroy their idyllic image of her father? Or should she carry the truth home with her to San Francisco and remain alone in this world? Whatever choice she makes during this London Christmas will forever change the future for both her and the family she can't bear to leave.